Lauren,

Well, well, if it isn't Randall Tanner's whelp come
home to roost. In the hunting lodge that's no more
yours than your daddy's. The land and everything
on it is Buck Tanner's, God rest his soul. And
before he passed, Buck made clear that no kin of
Randall's should ever live long on *Buck's* land.

So first a warning or two, to let you know you
ain't wanted around Tanner's Crossing.

After that, heaven help you.

Dear Reader

Silhouette Desire has a fantastic selection of novels for you this month, starting with our latest DYNASTIES: THE ASHTONS title, *Condition of Marriage* by Emilie Rose. Pregnant by one man…married to another, sounds like another Ashton scandal to me! *USA TODAY* bestselling author Peggy Moreland is back with a brand-new TANNERS OF TEXAS story. In *Tanner Ties,* it's a female Tanner who is looking for answers…and finds romance instead.

Our TEXAS CATTLEMAN'S CLUB: THE SECRET DIARY also continues this month with Brenda Jackson's fabulous *Strictly Confidential Attraction,* the story of a shy secretary who gets the chance to play house with her supersexy boss. Sheri WhiteFeather returns with another sexy Native American hero. You fell for Kyle in Sheri's previous Silhouette Bombshell novel, but just wait until you get to really know him in *Apache Nights.*

Two compelling miniseries also continue this month: Linda Conrad's *Reflected Pleasures,* the second book in THE GYPSY INHERITANCE—a family with a legacy full of surprises. And Bronwyn Jameson's PRINCES OF THE OUTBACK series has its second installment with *The Rich Stranger*—a man who must produce an heir in order to maintain his fortune.

Here's hoping this September's selections give you all the romance, all the drama and all the sensationalism you've come to expect from Silhouette Desire.

Melissa Jeglinski

Melissa Jeglinski
Senior Editor
Silhouette Desire

Please address questions and book requests to:
Silhouette Reader Service
U.S.: 3010 Walden Ave., P.O. Box 1325, Buffalo, NY 14269
Canadian: P.O. Box 609, Fort Erie, Ont. L2A 5X3

Peggy Moreland

TANNER Ties

Silhouette® Desire

Published by Silhouette Books
America's Publisher of Contemporary Romance

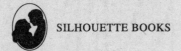 SILHOUETTE BOOKS

ISBN 0-373-76676-9

TANNER TIES

Copyright © 2005 by Peggy Bozeman Morse

Visit Silhouette Books at www.eHarlequin.com

Printed in U.S.A.

PEGGY MORELAND

published her first romance with Silhouette Books in 1989 and continues to delight readers with stories set in her home state of Texas. Winner of the National Readers' Choice Award, a nominee for the *Romantic Times* Reviewer's Choice Award and a two-time finalist for the prestigious RITA® Award, Peggy's books frequently appear on the *USA TODAY* and Waldenbooks's bestseller lists. When not writing, you can usually find Peggy outside, tending the cattle, goats and other critters on the ranch she shares with her husband. You may write to Peggy at P.O. Box 1099, Florence, TX 76527-1099, or e-mail her at peggy@peggymoreland.com.

Throughout our many moves over the years, we've been blessed with new friends, who made the adjustment of moving to a new area much easier. This book is dedicated to the McDaniels, a wonderful family, whom we met through a dog, of all things. Mike and Nancy, we treasure your friendship and look forward to spending many years as your "country" neighbors!

One

The dog looked a lot like an overgrown Benji…or might, if a person could see beyond the clods of dirt and burrs that matted its long, shaggy coat. At the moment, the animal was loping along the shoulder on the far side of the road, its tail a plume of tangled fur held high like a sail.

Lauren felt the familiar tug of her heart at the dog's bedraggled state and quickly stiffened her resolve. She couldn't take in a stray. She had all she could say grace over without adopting a dog that looked as if it could eat her out of house and home in a week's time. And she couldn't afford a vet bill, either, for the shots and checkup a stray would require.

No, she told herself, and forced her gaze away from the dog to the road ahead. She couldn't take the dog home with her. Even if she could afford to, where would she keep it? She and Rhena had carved out living space for themselves at the hunting lodge, but there wasn't room for a dog. Especially not for one the size of a small horse.

A truck pulled from a side road into the lane in front of her, snagging her attention. She slowed the car, her gaze going instinctively to the dog.

"Stay where you are," she urged under her breath. "Don't do anything stupid."

Oblivious to her concern or the danger that lurked only a few feet away, the dog chose that moment to dart out onto the road. Her heart in her throat, Lauren whipped her gaze to the rear of the truck, hoping that its lights would flash red, indicating that the driver had seen the dog and was braking. When the lights remained dark, she stomped on her own brakes and squeezed her eyes shut, praying the dog had made it across the road. When she opened her eyes, the truck was a good two hundred feet down the road…and the dog lay in a crumpled heap on the pavement.

She quickly parked her car at an angle to block the dog's body, so that another vehicle wouldn't hit it, then jumped out. Her legs shook as she rounded the hood of the car and dropped down to her knees next to the animal.

"Hey, buddy," she murmured, laying a hand gently on its side. "You okay?"

The dog lifted its head and gazed at her with the most pitiful-looking brown eyes she'd ever seen, then dropped its head back to the pavement with a muffled whimper.

Swallowing hard, she scooted closer. "I'm not going to hurt you, buddy," she assured the dog. "I just want to see how badly you're hurt."

Lauren winced, when she saw the pool of blood that was spreading on the road. She needed to turn the dog over in order to determine the severity of its injuries, but she was afraid to move it, for fear she would cause the animal more pain.

She glanced around, hoping to find a house nearby where she could go for help. But the country road stretched for miles in both directions, with nothing but pastureland lining its sides.

Hearing the sound of an engine in the distance, she scrambled to her feet and ran to stand in the middle of the road. She waved her arms over her head to stop the approaching truck. For a moment she thought the driver intended to speed right past her, but he finally slowed the truck, then drew to a stop and lowered his window.

"I need help," she gasped breathlessly. "Please."

Keeping his head down, the man snugged his cowboy hat lower over his brow, then opened his door and climbed down. "What's the problem?"

"Dog," she managed to get out, then shuddered, thinking of the blood, the pain in the dog's eyes. She grabbed the man's arm and tugged him behind her. "Over here. It's hurt."

When they reached the animal, she stood back, while the man hunkered down beside it. She could hear him murmuring to the dog as he ran his gloved hands over the animal's body, but couldn't make out what he was saying. She couldn't see the man's face, either, because of his hat, but she could see his mouth, which was set in a grim line.

She gulped and asked hesitantly, "Is it bad?"

"Bad enough. Pretty deep cut on his hip. Another on his rear leg. Can't tell if there are any broken bones."

She shifted her gaze to the man's hands and the leather work gloves that covered them. "Maybe if you took off your gloves you could get a better idea."

Ignoring her suggestion, he pushed his hands against his thighs and stood. "If you've got a blanket or something, I'll help you load him into your car."

She backed away, her eyes wide in horror. "Oh, no. I can't. It—it's not my dog."

His lips flattened. "Well, it's not mine, either."

"You could take him to the vet," she suggested hopefully.

"So could you."

"I...I can't." She gestured toward her car. "I've got groceries in my trunk. If I drive back to town now, they'll ruin."

He shrugged and headed toward his truck. "Then I guess the buzzards'll get him."

Stunned by his callousness, she stared a moment, then ran after him. "But you can't just leave him here to die!"

He opened his door. "Why not? That's what you're planning to do, isn't it?"

She glanced back at the dog and wrung her hands. "I'm new to Tanner's Crossing. Even if I didn't have groceries to worry about, I wouldn't know where to take him." She dug her hand in her pocket. "If it's the money you're worried about, I'll help with the expenses." She thrust a wad of bills at him. "Fifty dollars. It's all the cash I have with me."

He hesitated a moment, as if not wanting to bother with the dog, then heaved a sigh and reached behind his seat and pulled out a horse blanket.

"What are you going to do with that?" she asked, following him as he returned to the injured animal.

"Load him into my truck."

She hovered over the stranger, watching as he eased the blanket beneath the dog and picked it up. The dog let out a low whimper, the movement obviously painful. She ran ahead to open the passenger door of the truck, then stepped aside, giving the man the room he needed to lay the dog on the floorboard.

"You'll take good care of him, won't you?" she asked uneasily.

He tucked the blanket around the dog, then closed the door. "I'll see that he gets the care he needs."

Nodding, she offered him the money again. "I know it's not much, but it'll help with the vet's fees."

With his mouth set in a grim line, the man shoved her hand aside and rounded his truck. "Keep your money. Use it to buy yourself a new heart."

Arriving home fifteen minutes later and still fuming over her encounter with the stranger, Lauren dumped the last grocery sack onto the kitchen counter. "And when I offered him money, he wouldn't take it," she said, continuing to relate the incident to Rhena. "He told me to use it to buy myself a new heart! Can you believe the nerve of the guy?"

Rhena plucked a gallon of milk from the sack and headed for the refrigerator. "I don't know what you're so upset about. He took the dog, didn't he?"

"Yes, but—"

"And that's what you wanted him to do, wasn't it?"

"Well…yes."

Rhena set the milk in the refrigerator, then returned to the counter. "So what's your beef?"

"He was rude! He all but called me callous and heartless."

"What do you care what he thinks of you?"

"I don't."

Rhena pulled canned goods from the sack. "You're just feeling guilty because you didn't take the dog yourself."

"I can't afford to take in a stray. Even if I could, we don't have a place to keep it."

"So you did the next best thing. You found someone else to take the dog."

Lauren sagged her shoulders miserably. "Why doesn't that make me feel better?"

"Because you think he won't take as good care of the dog as you would."

She grimaced, because Rhena had spoken the truth. "You know me too well."

"Should. I've taken care of you since you were in diapers."

Lauren scowled, remembering the man's behavior. "The guy was weird. He wouldn't look me in the eye. Kept his hat pulled down low, so I couldn't see his face. He even had on gloves and refused to take them off when he examined the dog for broken bones."

"Smart man," Rhena said, with a nod of approval. "No telling what kind of diseases a stray might carry."

"Weird," Lauren repeated stubbornly. "Did I mention that he had on a long-sleeved shirt buttoned all the way up to his chin? Considering he had on work gloves, too, I'd say he's either extremely modest or part of some religious sect that considers exposing flesh a major sin."

"Maybe he was just trying to protect himself from the sun. People do that, you know. Skin cancer isn't anything to sneeze at."

"Why are you so determined to defend this guy?" Lauren asked in frustration.

"Why are you so anxious to hang him?" Rhena returned. "He took the dog, which is what you wanted him to do. You should be grateful." She waved an impatient hand at the other sacks of groceries. "Now forget about the dang dog and help me put these away. We've got work to do, and standing around yapping isn't going to get it done."

"How's the mutt doing?"

Luke glanced up at the sound of his boss's, Ry Tanner's, voice, then turned his attention back to the dog and finished spreading the ointment over the line of stitches that trailed down the animal's leg. "Better. Still got a long way to go, though."

"He's in good hands," Ry said. "You've got a gift with animals."

Frowning, Luke picked up a cloth and began wiping the ointment from his fingers as he stood. "There're times I wish I didn't."

Ry looked at him curiously. "And why is that?"

His frown deepening, Luke gestured to the dog. "I might've saved his life, but for what? His chances for survival are slim at best. If he doesn't end up as road-kill, some rancher is going to shoot him, thinking he's a danger to his livestock."

"Strays are a problem for ranchers," Ry reminded him. "We've lost our share of cattle to wild dogs. A rancher's only defense is to shoot the strays."

"Who should be shot are the city folks who dump their pets out in the country. Poor animals are just hungry and tryin' best they know how to survive."

"I can't argue that," Ry said. "But until someone comes up with a solution to the problem, people are going to continue to dump their pets in the country. There's no way to stop them. There are no fines or regulations outside the city limits. Pet owners know that and take of advantage of it."

Scowling, Luke screwed the cap back on the tube of ointment and set it on a shelf. "Doesn't make it right." He dragged his hands across the seat of his jeans and heaved a sigh. "Was there something special you needed? I'm about to head out. I'm supposed to meet Monty to mend some fencing."

"As a matter of fact, there's something I need to discuss with you." Ry followed Luke from the feed room out into the alleyway of the barn. "A cousin of ours has moved into the old hunting lodge. She's planning to convert it into some kind of bed and breakfast or something along that line. Never have quite understood what exactly. My brothers and I offered her our help, but she refused." He shrugged as they stepped outside into the sunshine. "She's stubborn. Always has been. But we're worried about her. She's had a tough time of it lately."

Luke stopped beside his truck and looked at Ry in puzzlement. "What's all this have to do with me?"

Ry reached into his shirt pocket and pulled out a newspaper clipping. "She advertised in the paper for a part-time handyman. We'd appreciate it if you'd apply for the job."

Luke stared at the clipping, his gut clenching in dread. "Is this a nice way of saying I'm fired?"

Ry choked a laugh. "Hardly. You know we couldn't run the Bar-T without you, Luke. We just need someone to keep an eye on our cousin. Look out for her. The job's part-time and probably short-term, which means, if you get the job, you'd work whatever days she needs you and work the rest of the time at the ranch. Once she no longer needs you, you'd be back here full-time."

Luke scratched his chin. "I don't know," he said hesitantly. "I'm not much on being around folks."

"I wouldn't ask if it wasn't important." His expression somber, Ry clapped a hand on Luke's shoulder. "We need your help, Luke. Ace, Rory, Woodrow, Whit—we've all talked about this, and we decided you were the best man for the job. You're good with your hands. Can fix almost anything that's put in front of you. But your most important qualifications are your honesty and your loyalty to the Tanners. We know that we can trust you to look after our cousin."

Luke wanted to refuse. Agreeing to the proposition would mean talking to a woman, spending time around one, something he avoided at all cost. But he owed Ry. If not for Ry and his skill as a surgeon, Luke might've lost the use of his hands, and without his hands…well, they might as well have shot him and put him out of his misery, 'cause he was no good without them.

"All right," he agreed reluctantly. "I'll apply for the job. But don't blame me if she turns me down," he added.

"And why would she do that?" Ry asked. "You're more than qualified for the job."

Luke tipped back his hat and pointed a finger at his face. "Most women find this a bit hard to look at."

Luke put off paying a visit to the Tanners' cousin until the next afternoon. He would've put it off longer, if Ry hadn't asked him at breakfast that morning if he'd talked to her yet. Knowing there was no sense in avoiding the "interview" any longer, he made the drive to the hunting lodge.

Upon the death of Buck and Randall Tanner's father, the Bar-T—the Tanner ranch—had been divided between the two brothers. Buck, the older of the two, had received the bulk of the land, and Randall had inherited the lodge and the five hundred acres of land surrounding it. Luke had heard that Buck, Ry's father, hadn't been pleased with the split, which was ridiculous, considering Buck had inherited the lion's share of the sizable Tanner estate. Rumor was, Buck had tried to buy the property from his brother and when Randall refused to sell, Buck had never spoken to him again.

Luke shook his head sadly as he parked his truck in front of the old lodge. Buck Tanner had been a stubborn man, one whose life was filled with more drama than all the soap operas on television put together. And he had been mean. He was probably rolling in his grave right now at the thought of his brother's daughter moving into the old lodge.

With a sigh, Luke climbed down from his truck, snugged his hat low over his brow and walked to the front door. Freshly turned earth marked a long trench that ran from the well house to the lodge, suggesting a plumber had recently laid new lines. Making a mental note to report the repairs to Ry, he rapped his gloved knuckles against the thick cedar door, then waited, silently praying that his knock wouldn't be heard and he could leave with a clear conscience, knowing he'd at least tried. He was just about to turn for his truck, when the door swung open with a creak.

"Can I help you?" a woman asked.

Luke stole a glance at the woman from beneath the brim of his hat and was surprised to find that she was a good deal older than he'd expected.

Keeping his gaze cast down, he drew the classified ad from his shirt pocket. "Yes, ma'am. I've come about the ad you ran in the paper."

She eyed him suspiciously. "Do you have any remodeling experience?"

"Not specifically," he admitted. "But I'm good with my hands. I can handle a saw and hammer well enough, and I can fix just about anything that's broke."

"Do you drink?" she asked bluntly.

He glanced up in surprise at the question, then quickly dropped his gaze again and shook his head. "I enjoy a cold beer every now and then, but I'm no alcoholic, if that's what you're asking."

"Do you have a police record?"

He bit back a smile at the woman's persistence, thinking the Tanner brothers were wrong about their cousin. There wasn't a doubt in Luke's mind that this woman could take care of herself. "No, ma'am. Last traffic ticket I received was for speeding, and that was a good five years ago."

Still eyeing him suspiciously, she stepped aside. "All right. You can come in."

He didn't look up at her but stepped inside, wondering if this meant he had the job. The room she led him into was the main room of the lodge and probably forty feet square. It was obvious that more repair work was going on inside, as the room was bare of any furnishings. Paper covered the floor and crackled with each step he took as he followed the woman across the room. The odd lengths of electrical wire scattered about indicated an electrician had been working on the wiring.

"Lauren is out back," she said, gesturing to a set of French doors. "Working on the porch. She's the one who'll decide whether or not to hire you."

Luke stared at the retreating woman in confusion. "You're not the one who placed the ad?"

She stopped and glanced over her shoulder. "No. Lauren did. Lauren Tanner. She's the owner." She gestured toward the doors again. "Go on out and talk to her. See what she has to say. Chances are she'll hire you. She could definitely use the help."

Before Luke had a chance to say anything more, the

woman stepped into another room and closed the door behind her.

Wishing he could head back to the ranch and forget his promise to Ry, Luke heaved a sigh and strode for the door. Once outside, the sound of hammering drew him to the far end of the porch. A pair of beat-up tennis shoes and denim-covered legs were his only view of the person swinging the hammer from a ladder perched against the roof of the house.

"Ms. Tanner?" he shouted, in order for her to hear him above the banging noise.

The hammering stopped and a head appeared below the edge of the roof. Luke bit back a groan when he found himself looking at the woman who had dumped the dog on him. The family resemblance was so strong, he was surprised he hadn't made the connection the day she stopped him on the road. She had the Tanner eyes, blue as a summer sky. And her hair was the same inky black as the Tanner brothers.

Although he was careful not to expose his face, she must've recognized him, too, because her lips thinned and her eyes narrowed. "Did you change your mind about taking my money?" she asked irritably.

"No, ma'am." He pulled the classified ad from his shirt pocket again. "I'm here about the job."

She hesitated a moment, then stomped down the ladder, making the metal rungs sing. "Have you done any remodeling before?"

"Yes, ma'am, though not on a regular basis."

Reaching the ground, she yanked off her gloves. "Do you have any experience with woodworking equipment?"

"Yes, ma'am."

"Masonry?"

"Some."

"What about roofing?"

He stepped out into the yard and looked up at the roof to judge his abilities. Finding it was a tin roof, he breathed a sigh of relief. Tin he could deal with. If it had been a tile roof, that would've been a different matter. "I can make what repairs are needed."

"What about water wells? Do you know how to deal with them?"

"I couldn't dig one, but I can keep a well pump running."

"Do you have any references?"

He panicked a moment, but decided honesty was the best policy, even if he did sort of stretch the truth a bit. "I've done work for the Tanner brothers. I suppose they'd vouch for me."

The mention of the Tanner brothers didn't seem to please her. Scowling, she stuffed her gloves into the rear pocket of her jeans. "The pay is minimum wage and the work back-breaking. Twenty hours a week is all I can afford, and when the remodeling's completed, the job is over. Understand?"

"Yes, ma'am. I do."

"I expect you here by seven each morning. It's cooler then. You can leave at noon, and not a minute sooner. I expect an honest day's work from you, and I won't accept sloppy craftsmanship. Any job worth doing is worth doing right."

"I don't have a problem with that."

"Do you have a preference for what days you work?"

He lifted a shoulder. "No, ma'am. Like I said, I'm flexible."

"Then we'll play it day by day. See what works best. You can start tomorrow. Seven sharp."

She started up the ladder and Luke turned away, figuring the interview was over and the job was his.

"How's the dog?"

He turned back, surprised that she cared enough to ask. "As good as can be expected, I guess."

"Were any bones broken?"

"No, ma'am. Took thirty-two stitches to close the wounds, but nothing was broken."

Her shoulders sagged in relief. "Thank God," she murmured, and started up the ladder again.

Anxious to leave, Luke headed for the side of the house.

"Hey!" she called, stopping him.

He glanced back over his shoulder. "Yes, ma'am?"

"You didn't tell me your name."

"Luke. Luke Jordan."

She opened her mouth as if she intended to ask him something else, but clamped her lips together and stomped up the ladder to the roof.

After his interview, Luke drove straight back to the Bar-T and knocked on the back door of the ranch house.

"Door's open!" Ry called.

Dragging off his hat, Luke stepped inside. Ry sat at the table, reading the evening paper. Kayla, Ry's wife, stood before the stove, stirring something in a pot. The aroma drifting from it made his mouth water.

She glanced over her shoulder and offered him a bright smile. "Hi, Luke. How're you doing?"

That she could look at him without wincing never ceased to amaze Luke. Never once had she shown any sign of disgust. Not even prior to the surgeries Ry had performed to repair the burns to his face and hands had she ever appeared repulsed by his scarring.

He offered her a smile in return. "Fine, ma'am." He turned his attention to Ry. "I got the job. Start tomorrow."

Ry set the newspaper aside. "Any problems?"

Luke shook his head. "Gave me the third degree but seemed satisfied with my answers. The older woman grilled me pretty hard, too."

"That would be Rhena," Ry explained. "She's worked for Lauren's family for years. If what we heard is correct, she was more of a mother to Lauren than an employee."

Luke knew nothing about Lauren or her family, so remained silent.

"How was she?" Ry asked. "Did she appear upset or worried about anything?"

Luke considered Ry's question for a moment, then shook his head. "She seemed all right to me. She was working on the roof above the back porch when I got there. Came down off the ladder to talk to me, then went right back up when we were done."

"How did the place look?" Ry asked curiously.

"I could tell that some repairs have been made. Electrical wiring's been replaced. Looked like a plumber's been there, as the ground around the septic system appeared freshly turned. But there's a lot more to be done."

Kayla bit back a smile as she joined Ry at the table. "You missed your calling, Luke. You should have been a detective."

He snorted a laugh. "I hardly think noticing a few new wires and freshly turned dirt qualifies me as a detective."

"I wouldn't have noticed those things," she replied, then glanced at her husband. "Would you, Ry?"

He shook his head. "Can't say that I would." He winked at Luke. "But since Luke did, that proves we chose the right man for the job."

Luke shuffled his feet a moment, curious to know about the Tanner brothers' relationship with their cousin but reluctant to ask. "I'm not trying to get in your business, Ry, but would you mind telling me why you want me to keep an eye on the woman?"

"I told you. She's our cousin, and we're worried about her."

"Yeah, but it seems it would be a heck of a lot easier for you or one of the others to just drop in on her every now and again and check on her."

"You're right," Ry agreed. "It would. Unfortunately, our father, Buck, made that impossible." He lifted his hands in a helpless gesture. "You know how Buck was, Luke. He alienated more people than most folks meet in a lifetime. He treated family even worse. After Randall, Lauren's father, refused to sell him the lodge, Buck disowned him. Cut him out of his life as if he never existed, and never spoke to him again. That was over twenty-five years ago." He shook his head sadly. "I don't know how much Randall told Lauren about his relationship with his brother, but whatever it was must have shed a bad light on us all, because she doesn't want anything to do with any of us.

"When we heard she was moving here," he continued, "Ace called her up, offered her our help. She turned him down flat. Said she didn't need any help from the Tanners. Rory tried again, shortly after she arrived in town. He dropped by the lodge to see her and he said it was like talking to a brick wall."

Though Luke knew what Ry said was probably true, it didn't ease his reluctance in spying on the woman. "I don't feel right doing this. Seems underhanded somehow."

Ry nodded. "I can understand why you might feel that way. But we're not asking you to do anything illegal. All we want is for you to make sure she's safe, that she doesn't want for anything."

Luke thought about that for a moment, then nodded. "Fair enough." He snugged on his hat and headed for the back door. He stopped in the doorway and glanced back. "I better warn you, though. I have a feelin' if she finds out I'm spyin' on her for y'all, she's gonna be madder than a wet hen."

Two

Lauren was surprised the next day when Luke arrived at seven sharp. She'd have bet the farm that he wouldn't show up at all…and had secretly hoped he wouldn't.

It bugged her that he'd applied for the job two days after their chance meeting on the road. Rhena kept insisting the two events were nothing but a coincidence. Since Lauren hadn't told Luke her name, revealed her address or said anything about needing to hire a handyman, she had to believe Rhena was right.

But it still bugged her.

She frowned as she watched him climb down from his truck. It bugged her, too, that he wore his hat low over his brow, kept his gloves on all the time and buttoned his shirt up to his chin. Rhena had said his manner of dress was probably a precaution against skin cancer. Lauren thought it was more likely that he was an escaped convict who feared detection. That made more sense, considering the way her luck with men was running lately.

When he headed for the front door, obviously not having seen her, she shouted, "Over here!"

He stopped and glanced her way, then strode for the side yard. "Mornin', ma'am."

She flapped an impatient hand at his old-fashioned manners. "Whatever." She gestured to the lumber stacked at the side of the house. "We need to move this around to the back porch. We'll be working there today."

Without a word, he hefted a large stack of boards to his shoulder and carried it to the rear of the house.

Lauren picked up a sack of nails and followed. "Some of the flooring on the porch needs to be replaced. There's a leak on the roof and the boards below have rotted."

He set the lumber down near the sawhorses she had set out, then straightened and peered up at the roof. "Wouldn't it make more sense to fix the roof first? If it rains, the floor'll just get wet again."

"Which is why *you're* going up on the roof and repairing the leak, while *I* replace the boards on the porch."

What she could see of his face turned a bright red. "I'll get right on it," he said, and started for the ladder.

Lauren felt a stab of remorse for her rudeness, but dispelled it by reminding herself that she was the boss. It was important that she establish the lines of authority early on. If she didn't, he might try to take advantage of the fact that she was a woman.

Grabbing a crowbar, she set to work, prying up the rotted boards and tossing them into a pile to discard later. As she worked, she could hear the solid thud of Luke's footsteps on the roof overhead and the screech of old iron as he pulled nails from the sheets of tin.

"Ms. Tanner?"

She lifted her head and wiped sweat from her brow. "What?" she asked impatiently.

"I'm going to need at least four sheets of tin to replace the damaged ones I've found so far. Maybe more. Do you have any on hand?"

She stifled a groan, wishing she'd thought to request tin when she placed her order with the lumberyard earlier that week. The owner charged her exorbitant delivery fees. Probably because her last name was Tanner and he assumed she could afford to pay whatever price he named. Hoping to avoid an extra delivery, she racked her brain, trying to remember if she'd seen any tin lying around.

"I think there are some extra sheets in the barn," she called to him.

She heard the thud of his footsteps as he crossed back to the ladder, then saw his boots appear on the top rail. The ladder shook beneath his weight as he clomped down. Upon reaching the ground, he angled his body in profile to her to avoid looking at her. "If it's all right with you, I'll check and see if they're in good enough condition to use."

It irritated her that he wouldn't look at her when he spoke to her, but it irritated her even more that she couldn't see his face.

"Fine," she snapped. "Look in the·loft. I think that's where I saw the tin."

She watched him walk away, her frown deepening. His gait was long and easy, his shoulders square. And his head was up, which added another level of irritation to her already miffed mood. He could look at the barn but not at her? The man was beyond weird.

And he was big. He had to be over six feet tall, since the top of her head hit him about chin level. He had wide shoulders and a broad chest that tapered to a slim waist and hips. His legs were long and muscled beneath his jeans, and he had what she'd heard referred to as a cowboy butt—nicely rounded and muscled—as well. His hair—or what she could see of it beneath his ever-present cowboy hat—was a sandy brown. Other than that, she had no idea what he looked like.

Frustrated by his secretive behavior, she attacked a rotted board and pried it up, taking pleasure in the grind of nails and splintering of wood as the board snapped free. She tossed it aside and crawled along the porch until she reached the next damaged board. In spite of the earliness of the morning, it was strenuous work and sweaty, but she relished the burn of muscle, the sense of accomplishment with each finished task. And she was grateful at the end of each workday for her weariness, knowing she'd be able to sleep that night and not toss and turn, haunted by old memories and worries over her future.

A loud crash had her snapping her head up, her gaze going to the barn. Fearing that Luke had fallen out of the loft, she leaped to her feet and ran. Inside the build-

ing she stopped to stare, her chest heaving, as she struggled to catch her breath. Luke stood in the alleyway,
looking down at a pile of tin, a shovel gripped between
his hands like a weapon.

"What happened?" she asked, pressing a hand to her
chest to still her heart's beating.

He braced the shovel against the ground and shook
his head. "Rattler. Must've been curled up between the
sheets of tin. When I pulled 'em down, he came down
with 'em."

Wrinkling her nose in distaste, she eased closer and
saw the rattlesnake—or what was left of it—on the
ground, and shuddered. "D-did he bite you?"

He puffed his cheeks and released a shaky breath.
"No, ma'am. Wanted to, though. I heard the rattle and
grabbed the shovel from the wall and whacked it before
it had a chance to strike."

She shifted her gaze to Luke and froze, noticing for
the first time that his hat was missing, which offered her
a clear view of the left side of his face. Crepey skin,
shades lighter than the rest of his face, covered a por-
tion of his cheek. A thin line of puckered flesh trailed
from his eyebrow up toward his hairline. That he'd suffered some type of injury was obvious. Exactly what
kind, she wasn't sure. The scarring wasn't hideous by
any stretch of the imagination, but she thought she understood now why he always kept his face hidden.

He glanced over and she found herself looking into
eyes colored a soft, warm brown. Kind eyes, she
thought. Gentle. The kind of eyes a woman could trust.
The kind she could fall into and drown.

When he realized she was staring at him, he quickly turned away and scooped his hat from the ground, his face stained a deep red. After snugging the hat down over his head, he took up the shovel again.

"As soon as I get rid of the carcass," he said, keeping his face averted, "I'll bring the tin up to the lodge and get to work on the roof."

It took her a moment to find her voice. She wanted to ask him what had happened to him, to tell him he shouldn't be ashamed of the scarring, that it wasn't that bad.

Instead, she said, "All right," and walked from the barn, leaving him to deal with the dead snake, and the questions to whirl in her mind.

That evening Lauren sat slumped in one of the Adirondack chairs on the lodge's front porch. Rhena sat beside her, shelling black-eyed peas. The rhythmic click of peas hitting the pan she held on her lap was a soothing sound in the darkness.

"What do you think happened to him?" Lauren asked thoughtfully.

"Who?"

"Luke. How do you think he got all those scars?"

"How the heck would I know? If you want answers, you'll have to ask him."

"I wanted to," Lauren admitted guiltily. "But I couldn't bring myself to ask him about something that he's obviously so self-conscious about."

Rhena snorted. "Since when has that stopped you from sticking your nose in somebody else's business?"

Lauren looked at her in surprise. "Are you saying I'm nosy?"

"Need I remind you about the day you asked Florence when her baby was due?"

Lauren pursed her lips. "I was eight years old. I thought anybody with a tummy was pregnant. Besides, all the household staff was wondering the same darn thing, including *you,*" she added. She jutted her chin defensively. "I saved y'all the embarrassment of asking."

"And cost Florence her job."

Lauren felt a prick of guilt, but quickly dispelled it. "Was it my fault she was sleeping with the gardener? Florence knew Dad's rules. 'Employees of the Tanner household shall not fornicate with other employees of same household.' I believe that was rule number five, which was preceded by, 'No employees of the Tanner household shall gossip about happenings within the Tanner home or about family members who reside in said home.'"

"Your father was a careful man and expected complete loyalty from his employees," Rhena replied judiciously. "There's nothing wrong with that."

Frowning, Lauren slumped farther down in her chair. "Easy for you to say. You didn't grow up with a bodyguard shadowing your every step."

"No. My parents were dirt poor. They didn't have anything anybody else would want, including me."

Lauren glanced uneasily at Rhena. "You think I'm spoiled, don't you?"

Rhena dropped her hands to her lap and looked at Lauren in disgust. "Now that's downright insulting. I had a hand in your raising, and I never spoiled you. Not once."

"My father did."

Pursing her lips, Rhena picked up another pod to shell. "He might've tried, but he didn't succeed. If he had, you would've run home with your tail tucked between your legs after you and Devon divorced, and let your daddy take care of you. But you didn't," she said with a nod of approval. "You took what you had left and put your back into it in order to survive. In my book, that's gutsy, not spoiled."

Reminded of the challenge she'd taken on, Lauren gazed out at the darkened landscape. "Daddy thinks I'm crazy for trying to turn the lodge into a business."

"The old fart," Rhena said grumpily. "He thinks everything's crazy that wasn't his idea."

Laughing softly, Lauren gave Rhena's arm an affectionate pat. "Oh, Rhena. What would I do without you?"

"You'd do just fine."

"I don't know that I would. You've been my rock ever since I can remember."

"You're stronger than you think, Lauren Tanner," Rhena lectured. "Life's dealt you some hard blows, but you've bounced back from every one of them, fists up and ready to fight."

"Bounced back?" Lauren repeated doubtfully. "Crawled is more like it."

"So it took you some time to recover. So what? The point is, you did. A weaker person would've curled up in a ball and given up. Not you. You grieved a little, sure. What woman wouldn't? But then you gathered up the pieces of your life and went on about the business of living."

Lauren suspected that Rhena was referring to more than her divorce. She was thinking of her mother's death, as well. Growing pensive, she turned to gaze at the darkness again. "I wish I knew why Mom did what she did."

"She was unhappy," Rhena said simply.

"Why?" Lauren asked in frustration. "She had a good life. A husband and children who loved her. A beautiful home and plenty of friends. What more could she have wanted?"

Rhena laid a hand on Lauren's arm. "Honey," she said gently, "some things just can't be explained. They just are." Drawing her hand back, she began to shell peas again. "Your mother was…fragile. She was when your father married her, and nothing he could do or say was going to change that. And believe me, he tried every way known to man to make her happy."

"Am I like her?"

Rhena looked at her in amazement. "Where did *that* come from?"

"Devon said I was. That I was impossible to please, just as she was."

Rhena huffed. "That's the biggest bunch of malarkey I've ever heard. Devon was the one to blame for the failure of your marriage. Never even tried. He was a taker, not a giver."

"Dad thinks I'm a fool for having given him access to my bank accounts."

"If he said that to you, then your daddy's the fool. Devon was your husband. You had no reason not to trust him."

"I do now," Lauren said wryly.

"Yes, but not then. You loved him. A woman should be able to trust the man she gives her heart to."

"'Should' being the operative word."

"Yes," Rhena agreed. "But just because one man disappoints you doesn't mean they all will."

Lauren shook her head. "Once burned was enough for me. I'll never let another man hurt me like that again."

Lauren worked alongside Luke most of the next morning, trimming the trees that surrounded the lodge. The chore was his idea, not hers. Since there wasn't enough tin for him to finish repairing the roof, he'd suggested trimming the tree limbs that grew over the lodge, which he claimed were responsible for most of the damage done to the roof. Once they started trimming, he'd insisted upon removing the dead limbs, as well, since, according to Luke, they posed a threat to anything and anyone below if they were to fall during a windstorm.

As she worked alongside him, dragging away the limbs he cut, she noticed that he kept his hat down and his face averted. It was no easy task, considering he was manning the pole chainsaw and had to keep his gaze on the tree overhead while cutting down limbs. Lauren had tried to ignore the awkwardness of his position, but after several hours of watching him, she totally lost her patience.

Dropping the limb she held, she snatched off his hat. "Enough is enough!" she cried angrily. "I know your face is scarred, so there's no point in trying to hide it from me any longer."

He clamped his jaw down and snatched his hat from her hand. "I wasn't trying to hide anything. Just trying to protect you, was all."

She tossed up her hands. "From *what?* I've seen cases of acne that were worse than the scars on your face."

He dropped his gaze and touched a hand to his cheek, as if to be sure the scars were still there. "Most folks find it hard to look at me."

"Well, I don't, and I would appreciate it if you'd look me in the eye when you speak to me, instead of ducking your head."

A muscle ticked on his jaw. "Yes, ma'am."

"You're not looking at me, you're looking at the ground."

He lifted his head and narrowed an eye at her. "Is that better?"

She jutted her chin. "Yes."

"Can we get back to work now, Ms. Tanner?"

"Don't call me Ms. Tanner. My name is Lauren."

He settled his hat over his head again, though this time in a more natural and comfortable position. "Yes, ma'am...*Lauren.*"

He put enough bite in her name to let her know that he might be willing to follow her orders, but that didn't mean he liked them. Deciding she'd pushed him far enough for one day, she picked up the limb she'd dropped and dragged it toward the brush pile, her nose in the air.

"Now that we've got that settled, let's get back to work."

Luke dipped the scoop into the feed bucket and measured out oats. He'd put in a solid five hours at the lodge, driven back to the Bar-T and put in six more, gathering steers and heading them to a new pasture. He was dead tired, but his mind was running like a colt fresh out of a stall.

He didn't know what to make of his new boss. First off, she was a Tanner, which meant she had to be rich as sin. Yet he hadn't seen any evidence of an extravagant lifestyle. No fancy clothes. No flashy jewelry. Even the car she drove wasn't what he'd expect to find a woman of her caliber driving. Although fairly new, the vehicle was modest at best…and totally unsuitable for where she currently lived. In his opinion, a person who lived in the country needed a truck or, at the very least, an SUV. Something tough enough to navigate rough terrain, and with enough storage capacity to haul whatever needed hauling.

And her current living conditions sure as hell weren't the Hilton. She and the woman who worked for her were all but camping out at the lodge and one of the cabins, having carved out living space for themselves amid the mess that went along with remodeling and construction. From what he could tell, the older woman took care of the household chores, while Lauren handled whatever grunt work needed doing. She worked right alongside Luke, doing chores better suited for a man, when she could just as easily have sat on the porch in the shade painting her nails and shouting out orders.

But the thing that confounded him most about the woman was her reaction to seeing his face. He'd known that she'd gotten a fairly good look at him the day before in the barn, when he'd lost his hat while killing the rattler. But the lighting was dimmer in the barn and he figured—based on the fact that she hadn't screamed or covered her eyes—that she hadn't seen how badly he was scarred. He might've gone on believing that, if she hadn't snatched off his hat this morning in full daylight and looked him square in the face, without flinching so much as a muscle. In fact, the only emotion she'd displayed was anger. That I've-had-all-of-this-I'm-gonna-take kind of anger that let a man know when a woman had reached the end of her rope.

Giving his head a shake, he dumped the oats into the trough and moved down the alleyway to the next stall. And that's what he couldn't figure. Why was she so hell-bent on him exposing his face? And why hadn't she cringed when she'd seen it? Hell, he was no fool. He hadn't been much to look at before the fire, and the scars it had left him with sure hadn't improved his appearance any. Ry Tanner might be a gifted plastic surgeon, but he was no magician. He couldn't put back what wasn't there in the first place.

Lauren, on the other hand, was a feast for the eyes. She had the same coal-black hair as the Tanner brothers, and the same deep-blue eyes. But all similarity to her cousins stopped there. She had a figure that made a man look twice, and a way of moving that made one stop and stare. Long-legged and slim-hipped, she walked with a purpose, chin up, arms swinging at her sides. And when she was studying something, a crease formed between her eyes and her lips puckered slightly.

He dumped the second measure of oats into the trough and released a lusty sigh. Those lips. Full, almost puffy looking and stained a natural rose. Beestung lips, his mother would've called them. *Kissable* was what he would call them.

He heaved another sigh, this one full of resignation, and strode to the next stall. Whether Lauren's lips were kissable or not, he'd never know. Even before the fire, a lady like her would've been out of his reach. She was a Tanner and he was…well, he was Luke Jordan, second son of a rodeo bum and short-order cook. He didn't have a pedigree, or any kind of degree, for that matter. He'd dropped out of high school in the eleventh grade and started cowboying full-time for any rancher who was willing to offer him a decent wage and a bunkhouse to sleep in.

No, he'd never know if Lauren's lips were kissable. Not firsthand, at any rate. Hell, she was so far out of his reach, he'd need a ladder to touch her toes.

A whine had him angling his head toward the feed room door.

With a smile tugging at one corner of his mouth, he set the bucket down and moved to unlatch the door.

"Hey, buddy," he said and dropped to a knee to give the dog's ears an affectionate rub. "How're you feelin' today?"

In response, the dog licked his hand.

His smile widening, Luke pushed to his feet. "Bet you'd like to stretch your legs a bit, after being cooped up so long, wouldn't you?" He patted a hand against his thigh, signaling the dog to follow him. "Come on, then. You can help me feed the horses."

The dog limped along behind him, pausing each

time he stopped to measure oats into a trough before moving on to the next stall. When they reached the last one, Luke hooked the feed bucket over a nail, then returned to the feed room. "Come on, buddy," he said, holding the door open. "It's time for me to head for the bunkhouse."

The dog sank down on his haunches and whined pitifully, not wanting to go back inside. Luke closed the door, then walked back to the dog and reached down to scratch its ears. "Don't blame you," he murmured softly. "I get pretty damn lonesome myself."

Rising, he slapped his hand against his thigh again. "Come on," he said, letting the dog know it was okay to follow him outside. "You can bunk with me tonight."

Once outside, Luke paused to look up at the sky. "Looks like we might get us some rain tonight," he said, then glanced over to see if the dog was listening and grinned when he saw that its ears were perked up. "Good sleepin' weather, right?"

In response, the dog let out a yip and darted for the bunkhouse. Laughing, Luke watched the dog run. Though he still favored his right rear leg, he was clearly on the mend. Pleased with the animal's progress, Luke stuck his hands in his pockets and continued to follow, wondering what Monty would say when he learned that Luke had invited the dog to spend the night with them.

As he neared the bunkhouse, a clap of thunder sounded in the distance and the wind picked up, scattering dead leaves across the path. He lifted his head to look at the sky again, and saw that dark clouds were roiling in from the north.

"Not just some rain," he amended, frowning at the boiling sky. "Looks like we're in for a real frog strangler."

He'd no sooner made the comment, than his thoughts segued to Lauren and the tin yet to be replaced on the roof of the lodge. A blowing rain would test the soundness of a good roof. No telling what kind of damage it would do to one as old as the one on the lodge. And if it hailed…well, she might as well kiss that roof goodbye, 'cause he seriously doubted that old tin could withstand the beating hail would give it.

What was worse, she was bound to lose her electrical power. Rural service usually went down in a bad storm and was slow to return after the weather passed over. He doubted there was a generator at the lodge or that Lauren would know how to run it if there was one.

He started toward his truck, intending to drive to the lodge and make sure she and the old woman were all right, but stopped just shy of reaching it. He couldn't go chasing over there to check on her, he told himself. She was a grown woman and capable of taking care of herself. She didn't need him fussin' over her, and doubted she'd appreciate him droppin' by uninvited.

But if something were to happen to her, then what? The woman was a greenhorn when it came to country life. She wouldn't know how to prepare for a storm and probably didn't have the supplies on hand to ride one out.

Firming his mouth, he strode to his truck. As he started to climb in, a bark stopped him. He looked over his shoulder and saw that the dog had followed. He glanced at the barn, weighing the time it would take to return the dog to the feed room. Sighing, he scooped up the dog and plunked him down on the passenger seat. The dog sat up, tongue lolling, and looked out the windshield.

Halfway to Lauren's, it started sprinkling. By the time Luke pulled up in front of the lodge, the rain was coming down so hard, he couldn't see two feet in front of the truck. He pulled a slicker from the back seat, shrugged it on, then yanked his hat down farther over his brow and opened his door. Before he could react, the dog leaped out of the truck. Within seconds his coat was plastered to his hide, making him look like an overgrown drowned rat.

As Luke clomped his way around back through the puddles already forming on the ground, he noticed that Lauren's car was gone. She'd probably hightailed it for town the minute she'd seen the storm clouds building, he thought. A good thing, in his estimation. Her absence also proved that she was a greenhorn. A person who couldn't handle a little rain had no business living in this neck of the woods and so far from civilization.

Among the building supplies stacked on the back porch, he found several rolls of plastic. Tucking one under his arm, he grabbed the ladder, carried it out into the rain and braced it against the edge of the roof.

"Stay," he instructed the dog, then climbed up the ladder, keeping his head down to protect his face from the stinging bullets of rain. He made quick work of rolling out the plastic and securing it with logs he borrowed from the firewood rack. By the time he reached the ground for the last time, he was soaked to the skin and winded.

Confident that the plastic would protect the lodge's

interior from water damage, he glanced toward the cabin where he knew Lauren stayed. Set five hundred or more feet from the rear of the lodge, it, too, was surrounded by trees. He could hear the screech of metal as the wind pushed the limbs across the cabin's tin roof. He wavered, wondering if he should put plastic on that roof, as well. With a sigh of resignation, he gathered up another roll of plastic and the ladder.

"Stay," he said to the dog again, who was standing under the lodge's back porch, watching him expectantly. The dog looked from him to the rain and sank down on its haunches.

Smart dog, Luke thought, as he made his way to the cabin.

He was halfway across the cabin's roof, when he heard a commotion below. Wondering what was going on, he slid to the edge of the roof and peered down. Lauren stood in front of the cabin, wearing a yellow raincoat and looking up at him from beneath its hood.

"What do you think you're doing?" she shouted, to be heard over the pounding rain.

"Puttin' plastic over the roof," he yelled back. "Almost done."

"You might have asked first."

"Didn't know you were here. Car's gone."

"Rhena went to town for groceries."

Damn fool woman, he thought, and shifted to start down the ladder. "I better go and look for her," he said. "Roads flood when we get this much rain in such a short time."

"That's not necessary," she called back, stopping

him. "She called earlier. Said she's staying in town with Maude until the storm is over."

Knowing Maude, Luke thought, Rhena probably didn't have much say in the matter. The owner of the local grocery store and the biggest gossip in town, Maude bossed everybody around, no matter what their age.

With a sigh he stepped onto the roof again. "Get back inside and out of the rain," he ordered.

"You can't tell me what to do!"

He paused, sure that he'd misunderstood, then moved back to the edge of the roof and saw that she was still standing in the rain, glaring up at him, her hands fisted on her hips. "Then stand there and drown," he told her. "Makes me no nevermind."

Muttering curses under his breath, he picked up a log, dropped it over the plastic to secure it, then tugged the sheet, walking backward, to spread it out more. He was bending to pick up another log, when he caught a flash of movement out of the corner of his eye. Lauren had grabbed the plastic roll and was slip-sliding her way across the roof, dragging it behind her.

Stubborn woman, he thought irritably. She was going to slip on the slick tin and fall and break her neck…if lightning didn't strike her first.

Well, if she did fall, that was her problem, he told himself, and continued to lay out plastic. She obviously didn't have the good sense God gave a goose.

Amazingly, they finished laying out the plastic without incident, then Luke followed Lauren down the ladder to the ground. Rain was streaming down his face and dripping off his chin as he folded the ladder, preparing to leave.

Her stance resentful, Lauren watched him, her arms hugging her waist. "You can add a couple of hours to your time sheet."

He dragged a hand down his face, sluicing off water, before lifting the ladder to his shoulder. "I didn't do it for the pay."

"Oh. Well," she said, obviously flustered. She frowned a moment, then gestured toward the cabin. "The least I can do is offer you a towel to dry off with."

"Thanks, but I better go. I've got—"

Before he could explain that he had the dog with him, the animal in question came bounding toward them on his three good legs, barking like a maniac.

At the sound, Lauren whirled. Her eyes went wide when she recognized the dog, and she dropped to her knees and opened her arms. The dog leaped up, planting its front paws on her shoulders and licking her face.

Laughing, she tried to dodge his exuberant greeting. "Just look at you!" she cried. "If I didn't know better, I'd never believe you were almost a greasy spot on the road."

Luke eased closer, surprised by her obvious delight in seeing the dog. "Another week or so and he'll lose the limp."

She glanced up at him, her face wreathed in a smile. "That vet you took him to must be one talented guy."

Luke dropped his gaze. "Uh…I never took him to the vet."

She looked at him curiously. "But I thought you said he required stitches?"

"Thirty-two in all."

"If a vet didn't stitch him up, who did?"

"Me."

"*You?*"

He scowled at the doubt in her voice. "I've worked around animals most of my life. He isn't the first one I've patched up."

Before she could reply, the first flash of lightning ripped the sky, followed by a deafening clap of thunder. Lauren quickly pushed to her feet. "We better get out of this storm."

"Yeah. Better." Luke slapped a hand against his thigh, signaling the dog to follow. "Come on. Let's hit the road."

Lauren dropped a protective hand on the dog's head. "Come inside and dry off first."

Luke shook his head. "'Preciate the offer, but I need to get the dog out of the weather."

"He's welcome to come in, too."

"But he's wet and muddy and smells like dog."

Laughing, Lauren gave the dog's ears an affectionate rub. "He is a dog. What should he smell like?"

Luke watched her head for the cabin door, the dog trotting happily along at her side. With no other choices left to him, he followed.

Three

The interior of the cabin was dark as a cave. Luke had been right in assuming Lauren would lose electrical power during the storm.

"Give me a second to light some candles," she said, "then I'll get you a towel."

He remained just inside the door and stripped off his dripping slicker, then toed off his muddy boots. He heard the scrape of a match and saw the burst of a small flame. With her hand cupped around it, Lauren leaned to touch the flame to a wick. The flame burned brighter, illuminating her face. She moved her hand to light a second candle, a third. After lighting them all, she straightened with a sigh, pushed back the hood of her jacket and shook out her hair.

He couldn't help but stare. God, she's beautiful, he

thought. In the candlelight, her hair gleamed like black satin and her cheeks like dew-kissed roses.

She glanced his way and gave him an apologetic smile, as she removed her raincoat. "I'm sorry I can't offer you hot coffee. The electricity's off."

"I figured you'd lose power during the storm."

"I can offer you a dry towel, though. Give me a sec and I'll get you one."

He watched her pass through an open doorway into another room. He heard her scuffling around inside and figured she was changing clothes. She appeared moments later, wearing a butter-yellow sweatsuit, a towel wrapped around her head, turban-style. She was carrying a stack of fluffy towels and handed him one, then dropped down on the sofa and opened the remaining one over her lap.

Smiling at the dog, she patted the towel. "Come on, Buddy. Let's get you dried off."

In the midst of drying off his own face, Luke slowly lowered the towel. "Buddy?" he repeated dully.

Her expression turning sheepish, she scrubbed the towel over the dog's head. "Sorry. Habit. I've probably had five pets in my lifetime, and I've named every one of them Buddy." With a shrug she wiped the towel over the dog's back. "So, what did you name him?"

He eased closer. "Didn't. I just call him…buddy."

She lifted her head and looked at him in surprise. "Really?" She shifted her gaze back to the dog and smiled. "Then, I guess Buddy's your name. Is that all right with you?"

In answer, he licked her full on the mouth.

Laughing, she dragged the back of her hand across her lips. "And isn't that just like a man? Trying to French kiss a woman on the first date." She quickly dried the dog's legs, then leaned back to inspect him. "You still look half-drowned, but that's the best I can do." She cocked her head. "How about a treat?"

The dog barked once, then plopped down on his haunches, his tail waving like a metronome.

"Such good manners," she praised as she rose. "How about you?" she asked, glancing Luke's way as she passed him on her way to the kitchen. "Are you hungry?"

Luke stared, adding yet another contradiction to the list of assumptions he'd made about Lauren. From the moment he met her, he'd pegged her as a coldhearted bitch. Yet, here she was making over the dog like he was a long-lost relative.

"Luke?" she repeated. "Would you like something to eat?"

He gave himself a shake. "No. No, ma'am. I'm fine."

With a shrug, she entered the kitchen.

"Would you mind lighting the wood in the fireplace?" she called to him. "I was making a fire when I heard you up on the roof."

"Sure thing." He hooked the towel over the back of his neck, then picked up the box of matches she'd left on the hearth. He struck one and touched the flame to the twists of paper she'd already placed between the logs. By the time she returned with a tray, he had a small fire burning.

"Have you used the fireplace before?" he asked, wondering belatedly if it was safe.

She placed the tray on a trunk in front of the sofa, then sat down. "No, but I had it checked. It's sound and draws well."

Relieved, he watched her offer Buddy a wiener. He couldn't help but smile when the dog all but inhaled the treat, then looked at her expectantly, as if waiting for more.

"In a minute," she promised. "You need to let that one digest first. You can take off your shirt, if you want, and hang it in front of the fire to dry."

It took Luke a moment to realize that she was talking to him and not the dog. He quickly shook his head. "Thanks, but I'm fine."

She gave him a doubtful look before breaking a wiener in half and offering one of the pieces to Buddy. "I promise you won't shock me. I've seen a man shirtless before."

She hadn't seen *him* shirtless, Luke thought. "I'm fine," he said again.

She shrugged as she fed Buddy half of the wiener. "Whatever floats your boat." She pushed the tray toward Luke. "I brought you a glass of brandy."

Luke sank down on the hearth and eyed the snifter of brandy warily, sure the fragile glass would snap in two if he so much as touched it. "I'm not much of a drinker," he said, hedging.

"Go on," she urged. "It'll take the chill off."

Knowing that refusing again would create more of a scene than simply drinking the stuff, he reached for the snifter with a sigh of resignation. On his first attempt, his nose bumped the narrow rim of the glass. Anxious to get this over with, before he broke the fragile glass or made a complete fool of himself, he tossed back half the contents. He held the liquid in his mouth a moment, trying to remember if he'd ever drunk brandy before. It wasn't a pleasant taste, he thought. Not necessarily *un*-pleasant. Just not his usual beer. He swallowed, then gaped, as fire streaked down his throat.

He glanced over at Lauren and saw that she was watching. He swallowed again and released a breath, amazed when flames didn't shoot from his mouth.

"Now I know why St. Bernard dogs carry a little keg of this stuff around their necks," he said wryly. "It'll definitely get the heart pumping again."

Chuckling, she fed the other half of the wiener to the dog. "I told you it would warm you up."

"It did that, all right." Feeling a bit more relaxed, he stretched out his legs, crossing his feet at the ankles, and watched as Lauren stroked the dog's head.

"How did you get the scars?"

He tensed at the unexpected question, then forced his shoulders to relax. "Burns. Got 'em in a barn fire."

"Were you trapped inside?"

He didn't detect any horror in her expression or morbid curiosity in her tone. "No. I was trying to get the livestock out."

"Did you succeed?"

"Yeah. One horse was hurt, but he's fine now. The rest just had a little hair singed off."

"And you were injured trying to save them."

He lifted a shoulder. "I couldn't just let 'em burn to death. They were locked in stalls, with no way out."

She studied him, while continuing to stroke the dog's

head. "That's why you won't take your shirt off, isn't it? It's because you have scars on your chest and back."

He set his jaw and looked away, refusing to answer. Before he knew what was happening, she was stooped over him and unbuttoning his shirt.

He batted at her hands. "What are you doing?"

She freed one button and started on a second. "Taking off your shirt. You're soaking wet and too stubborn or full of pride to do it yourself, so I'm going to do it for you."

He clamped a hand over her wrist. "Now wait a damn minute," he began.

Before he could stop her, she touched a finger to a scar that cut a lazy *S* across his sternum.

"Oh, Luke," she murmured, then lifted her gaze to his.

He didn't know if it was the warmth of her flesh touching his or the compassion he found in her eyes that did it, but whatever it was, it closed his throat up tight.

"Does it hurt?" she asked softly.

He shook his head and managed to find his voice. "Not anymore."

"How did it happen?"

"A beam fell as I was leading the last horse down the alleyway. I dodged it, but sparks flying from it set my clothes on fire. I guess I kinda lost my head, 'cause I took off running, like that could extinguish it. Ry was outside and he tackled me, rolled me on the ground."

"Ry Tanner?"

Too late, Luke realized his mistake in mentioning the Tanner name.

"I was working for the Tanners at the time," he said evasively.

She balled her hand into a fist and turned away. "I hope you sued them for all they're worth."

"It wasn't their fault."

She whirled to face him. "You were on their property and in their employ."

"Yeah, but I was the one who went into the burning barn. Nobody put a gun to my head and made me do it."

"It doesn't matter," she said angrily. "What you did was brave and totally selfless. You were—" She stopped and narrowed her eyes. "Since you were able to come to work for me, I suppose that means they fired you, once you were out of the hospital."

Luke racked his brain, trying to think of a response that wouldn't reveal that he was still working for the Tanners.

"I have no complaint with the Tanners," he finally said. "They took good care of me. Saw that I got the medical care I needed."

"No doubt to avoid a lawsuit."

When he would have contradicted her, she held up a hand. "Please don't defend them. They don't deserve your loyalty. The Tanners—or Buck's branch of the tree, at least—are nothing but a bunch of lying, conniving, self-serving men who will do anything to further their own gain."

Luke wasn't sure what to say. If he continued to argue with her, he was bound to end up revealing his association with the Tanner brothers. But failing to defend them made him feel like a heel. He finally decided a neutral position was best.

"I disagree," he said. "But I won't argue the point

with you anymore. You're entitled to your opinion, same as I am to mine."

"Shortsighted as it is," she grumbled, then fluttered an impatient hand. "Take off your shirt and I'll spread it out to dry."

He flattened a hand against his chest. "Shirt's fine just where it is."

She lifted a brow. "Would you rather I removed it for you?"

Knowing she wouldn't hesitate to do so, he tugged the shirttails from his jeans and shrugged out of the shirt, scowling all the while.

She draped the proffered shirt over her arm, then opened her hand.

He looked up at her in frustration. "What?"

She wiggled her fingers. "The gloves. Cough them up, cowboy. They're wet, too."

Grimacing, he tugged them off, slapped them over her palm, then quickly slid his hands beneath his thighs. "Has anyone ever told you you're bossy?"

Her smile smug, she laid the gloves on the hearth. "No, I don't believe anyone has."

"Well, let me be the first. You're bossier than an old cow."

She picked up the other snifter of brandy from the tray and took a dainty sip as she sank down on the sofa.

"You know," she said thoughtfully, studying him over the glass's rim. "I'll bet you're a lot more conscious of your scars than anyone else."

He snorted. "I'm not blind. I've seen how people look at me."

"What people?"

Uncomfortable, he rose and began to pace, unsure if her probing questions or the heat at his back were responsible for his discomfort. "Folks around town. Not that I blame them. I'd probably gawk, too."

"Oh, for heaven's sake," she fussed. "The way you talk, a person would think you looked like Frankenstein."

"Damn close."

"Would you stop!" she cried, then pointed a stiff finger at the cushion next to her. "And sit down. You're making me dizzy with all that pacing."

Scowling, he flopped down on the sofa as far away from her as he could get and folded his arms across his chest. "Happy now?"

"Ecstatic."

He shot her a sour look, then turned his face away, determined to ignore her.

As if sensing Luke's mood, Buddy wiggled his way past Lauren's legs and sat down at Luke's feet. Luke tried to ignore the dog, but Buddy refused to let him. He bumped Luke's arm with his nose and whined low in his throat.

With a sigh Luke dropped a hand to the dog's head and rubbed.

"I don't know why you insist on wearing gloves all the time," Lauren said. "Your hands don't look that bad."

Though the desire to hide his hands was strong, Luke kept rubbing the dog's head. "Would you mind finding something else to talk about other than my scars?"

"All right," she said agreeably. "Tell me about yourself."

He kept his gaze on the fire. "Nothing to tell."

"Sure there is. Everybody's got a history. Have you always lived in Tanner's Crossing?"

"Here or close by."

"What about your parents? Do they still live here?"

"Both are dead."

"Oh. Sorry." She frowned, then tried again. "Brothers and sisters?"

"One brother. Haven't seen him in years. Lives in Wyoming, last I heard."

"Married?"

He frowned at her, then turned his gaze back to the fire. "No."

"Never?"

"Never."

"Your turn."

He glanced her way. "For what?"

"To make conversation."

He shifted his gaze back to the fire. "I'm not much on talkin'."

"Try it. You might find you like it. You can start by asking me where I'm from."

He was willing to do just about anything to take the focus off him. "Where?"

"Dallas. I lived there all my life, before moving here."

When he said nothing more, she heaved a sigh. "My father is living. My mother passed away several years ago, and I have one brother, whom I see only when his schedule allows. His business takes him all over the world, so that isn't very often."

"Married?"

She beamed. "See? Making conversation isn't so hard to do."

"You didn't answer my question."

"Oh. Right. Once. Badly. Divorced about six months ago."

"Any kids?"

"No."

"So what brought you to Tanner's Crossing?"

She lifted her hands, indicating the cabin and all that stood beyond it. "This. My father gave me the property several years ago. After the divorce…well, let's just say I needed a new start."

"What are you plannin' to do with the place?"

"At first, I'm going to lease to hunters during hunting season. I have two groups of archers booked for the second week of October, and four groups of dove hunters for the end of October." She shuddered, as if feeling the weight of the time constraints she was under. "And here it is September already. Less than six weeks to go."

"And after hunting season is over?"

She lifted a shoulder. "I'll lease out rooms or cabins to whomever. Kind of like a bed-and-breakfast. Eventually I hope to attract businesses who need a place to hold small conferences, couples who want a country wedding. That type of thing."

"Sounds like a lot of work to me."

"It will be, I'm sure. If I make my deadline," she added with a frown. "I imagine this rain is going to slow the remodeling down."

"Maybe not. Just focus on the interior until the ground dries up."

"I intend to. That's why I've been working outside this past week." She sighed wearily. "But there's so much yet to be done."

"Like what?"

"Besides finishing the roof repairs, everything needs sprucing up. The grounds around the cabin and lodge need a good grooming. All the windows need to be cleaned, inside and out. The outdoor furniture needs new coats of stain before they can be set out for the guests to use."

He gave her a doubtful look. "The hunters won't care about any of that stuff. All they're interested in is what game's available to shoot."

"At the time, perhaps. But most of them are businessmen and I want them to see that the lodge has the amenities and charm to meet more than just their hunting needs."

Though Luke couldn't imagine the lodge being used for anything other than its original purpose—a *hunting* lodge—he thought it best to keep his opinion to himself.

"By spring," she continued, "I hope to have an area of the grounds prepared where weddings can take place. Nothing fancy," she clarified. "Just a backdrop, really. All the embellishments can be added to suit a bride and groom's particular taste."

He studied her curiously. "Have you ever done anything like this before?"

"Not professionally," she admitted reluctantly. "But I've had plenty of experience hosting elaborate parties. The basics are the same. The type of event planned will determine the details involved. Prior planning and organization are—"

A loud crash and the sound of shattering glass behind them, had her screeching. Luke grabbed her and dragged her down on the sofa, protecting her body with his. Buddy leaped up and raced to the door, barking furiously.

"What's happening?" she whispered fearfully.

"I don't know," Luke replied, "but I intend to find out." He lifted his head and peered over the back of the sofa. Slivers of glass shimmered like ice on the wood floor. "Window's busted," he reported.

"But…how?"

His gaze settled on a rock. "Somebody threw a rock through it." Setting his jaw, he leaned to blow out the candles, then rolled off her and to his feet. "Do you have a gun?"

She looked up at him, wide-eyed. "N-no. I hate guns."

He picked up his boots. "Figures," he muttered, as he tugged them on. "Stay right here," he ordered. "I'll be right back."

She popped to a sitting position. "Where are you going?"

He grabbed his slicker and opened the door. "To find whoever busted that window. Keep your head down," he instructed. "I shouldn't be long."

Once outside, he studied the area around the cabin as he shrugged on his slicker. Unable to see anything through the darkness and rain, he stepped off the porch and headed for the lodge, keeping to the shadows beneath the trees. He used the occasional flash of lightning to examine his surroundings, but found no evidence of an intruder.

When he reached his truck, he opened the driver's side door and pulled his shotgun from beneath the seat.

Again he paused and looked around, listening. Still hearing nothing but rain, he worked his way back to the cabin, winding through the cover of trees. He would've preferred to do a more intensive search, but the thought of leaving Lauren alone and unprotected in the cabin didn't sit well with him.

He stopped on the porch and shook his head, removing as much of the rain as possible, then stepped inside the cabin and propped his gun beside the door. With the dwindling fire offering the only illumination, the room was all but dark.

"Lauren?" he called softly.

Her head appeared above the back of the sofa. "Did you see anything?" she asked uneasily.

He shook his head as he peeled off his slicker. "Nothing. But it's so dark, I could barely see my hand in front of my face."

She rose from the sofa, her eyes wide with fear. "Who would do something like this?"

He hooked his slicker over a peg by the door and headed for the fireplace. "Don't know." He gathered a couple of logs from the rack and added them to the fire. "Have you had any problems before?"

Frowning thoughtfully, she joined him at the hearth. "Not that I'm aware of," she said slowly, then held up a finger, her eyes going wide. "Wait a minute. One morning last week the gas tank in my car was empty. I was sure that I'd filled it just a couple of days before when I was in town, but thought maybe I was mistaken." She glanced over at Luke. "I suppose someone could've siphoned the gas."

"Could've," he agreed. He held his hands out to the fire, seeking the warmth. "Is there anyone you know who might want to harm you?"

She slanted him a look. "Other than the Tanners?"

He flattened his lips. "The Tanners wouldn't hurt you."

"So you say," she replied sourly, then shook her head. "And to answer your question, no, I can't think of anyone. I haven't lived here long enough to make any enemies, or friends, for that matter."

She picked up the towel he'd left on the hearth earlier and pressed it against his chest. "Dry off. You're wet."

He wiped the towel across his chest. "Maybe you should consider staying with the Tanners. At least for tonight. I could drive you there."

She choked a laugh, then shook her head. "No, thank you. I'd feel safer here than with any one of them."

Frustrated, he hooked the towel over his neck. "You can't stay here. Whoever busted the window could still be out there."

"I'll lock the door."

He gave her a droll look. "Like that's gonna help. The window's already broken. Anybody who wants in could crawl right through."

She folded her arms across her chest. "I'm not leaving. I refuse to allow anyone to frighten me away from my own home."

"This isn't about being scared. It's about being safe. You don't have a gun to protect yourself."

"I wouldn't know how to shoot it if I did."

"Which proves my point. You don't have any business staying here alone."

"I'm *not* leaving."

He dragged the towel from around his neck and dropped it on the hearth. "Fine. Then I'll stay here with you."

Her eyes widened. "You most certainly are not!"

"Sorry, but I am." He gestured to the sofa. "I'll bed down in here. We'll need to cover that broken window. Wood would be best, but plastic will do for now. Do you have any duct tape?"

"Yes, and you're not staying."

"Where do you keep it?"

"In the kitchen drawer. You're not staying," she said again.

He stooped to light a candle, then picked it up and headed for the kitchen. Lauren charged after him. "You're not staying," she said angrily.

Ignoring her, he yanked open a drawer, closed it and opened another. Finding the tape, he carried it back to the den. "We can use a piece of the plastic left from the roof to cover the window."

She turned for the door. "I'll get it."

He caught her arm and pulled her back. "*I* will."

On the porch, he pulled a knife from his pocket and cut off a wide piece of plastic, then stepped back inside the cabin and shoved the plastic into her hands. "You hold it up against the window, while I put on the tape."

Though he could tell from the tightness of her mouth that she didn't like taking orders from him, she held the plastic up as instructed. Luke made quick work of applying the tape. When he was finished, he gestured toward the bedroom. "Go on to bed. I'll bunk down in here."

When she opened her mouth to say something, he held up a hand. "No sense arguin'. I'm not leavin' you here alone."

She glared at him a full three seconds, then spun on her heel and marched to her room, slamming the door behind her. He listened to her banging around inside for a minute, then the door opened and a quilt and pillow came sailing out. They had no sooner hit the floor than the door slammed again.

With a woeful shake of his head, he picked up the bedding, then began to strip off his wet clothes. He got down to his underwear, realized they were as wet as his jeans, and peeled them off, too. Covering himself with the quilt, he stretched out on the sofa and folded his arms beneath his head. He heard the click of Buddy's paws on the floor, then the dog's sigh as he settled on the floor next to the sofa.

Though exhausted, Luke lay awake, listening to the muffled sound of movements that came from the other room. Knowing Lauren was changing clothes, he closed his eyes and tried not to think about what she was doing or what she might look like unclothed. But in spite of his good intentions, a fairly good image formed in his mind. Long legs, creamy skin, small, full breasts.

Would her nipples be dark or a rosy pink? he wondered, then groaned and squeezed his eyes tighter shut. He couldn't think about that. Wouldn't. If he did, he'd be up all night.

He was on the edge of sleep, in that hazy world between unconsciousness and consciousness, when he heard the bedroom door creak slowly open. He tensed, but didn't open his eyes.

"Buddy," he heard her whisper. "Come here, Buddy. You can sleep with me."

Buddy lumbered to his feet and padded across the room, his nails clicking on the wooden floor.

"Good dog," she whispered.

The creak of the door closing let him know that both Lauren and Buddy were on the other side.

Biting back a smile, he shifted to his side and nestled his head into the pillow.

The woman wasn't quite as brave as she wanted him to believe.

Four

When Lauren awakened, sunshine was streaming through her bedroom window. She lay in bed for a moment, her mind dulled by sleep, thinking that something wasn't right. Something was missing. But what? She sat up straight, remembering that Buddy had slept with her.

"Buddy?" she whispered, looking frantically around. She swung her legs to the floor. "Buddy!" she whispered more loudly. When the dog didn't respond, she stooped to peer under the bed. Not finding him there, she grabbed her robe and tugged it on as she hurried from her room.

He wasn't in the den, either. Nor was Luke. The quilt she'd given him was folded neatly on the sofa and she smelled the distinct odor of coffee. Keeping her footsteps light, she tiptoed to the kitchen, expecting to find Luke sitting at her kitchen table, enjoying a cup.

But the kitchen, too, was empty.

Hearing a bark, she retraced her steps and opened the front door. With Buddy at his side, Luke stood about halfway between the cabin and the lodge, dressed in the clothes he'd worn the day before. The tail of his shirt was out and his hair was mussed from sleep. While she watched, he reached his arm back to throw a stick. When he released it, Buddy took off at a three-legged run, caught the stick in the air and brought it back to Luke.

Grinning, Luke stooped to rub the dog's ears. "Good boy, Buddy," she heard him say. Buddy barked once sharply, then waited expectantly. "Aren't you tired yet?" Luke asked, then chuckled when Buddy barked again. "Okay. I get the message." He drew his arm back again, preparing to throw. "Farther this time, okay, boy?"

He released the stick and it sailed through the air, turning end over end. Buddy raced off, his enthusiasm for the game evidenced by his excited barking.

"Won't he hurt himself running like that?" Lauren called uneasily.

Luke glanced over his shoulder. When he saw that she was wearing a robe and nightgown, he quickly looked away, his face flaming a bright red. "No. Exercise will do him good."

Amused by his embarrassment, Lauren crossed to the edge of the porch and braced a shoulder against a post. "Did you sleep all right?"

"Fine," he said, but kept his back to her.

"Would you like some breakfast?"

"I had some coffee."

"That's not food. Come inside and I'll make you something to eat."

He took the stick from Buddy and threw it again, managing to keep his back to her. "No rush. Go ahead and get dressed first."

She bit back a smile, enjoying his discomfort. "I *am* dressed."

The red spread to the tips of his ears, but he didn't say anything more.

Chuckling, Lauren went back inside. After putting on her clothes, she returned to the porch.

"It's safe to come inside now," she called to him. "I'm decent."

He threw the stick again. "I'm really not all that hungry."

She stepped off the porch. "Oh, for heaven's sake, Luke," she fussed as she marched across the yard, "you have to eat something."

"I wouldn't want to put you to any trouble."

She grabbed his arm. "I assure you, you're not." She gave him a tug. "Now, come inside. You can wash up while I make breakfast."

She had to half drag him to the cabin and didn't release him until they were inside.

She gestured toward her room and the bathroom beyond. "Washcloths and towels are in the cabinet beneath the sink. Help yourself to whatever you need."

While Luke cleaned up, she fried bacon and scrambled eggs, relieved that the electricity was back on and she didn't have to attempt cooking over the fireplace.

She was pulling a pan of biscuits from the oven when Luke returned to the kitchen. His shirt was tucked neatly into his jeans, and his hair was wet and slicked back from his face.

She straightened, lifting a brow. "Well, don't you look nice."

Self-conscious, he dragged a hand over the stubble on his cheek. "Could use a shave, I 'magine."

Biting back a smile, she crossed to the table. "You look fine." She set the pan of biscuits on a hot pad, then fluttered her hand. "Have a seat. Everything is ready."

He stood until she was seated, then sat opposite her, mimicking her movements as she spread her napkin over her lap.

"If you'll order the glass, I can replace that window for you," he said helpfully.

Reminded of the breakage, as well as the cost, she had to work at keeping her smile in place. "I'll add it to my list of items the lumberyard is delivering next week."

"You won't want to wait on a delivery. That window needs to be replaced today."

"We covered it with plastic. It'll be fine."

"But—"

"Deliveries are expensive," she said, cutting him off. She offered him the platter of eggs. "I appreciate your concern, but the glass will just have to wait."

Though she could tell he wanted to argue with her, he accepted the platter in silence.

"I suppose we'll need to check and see what damage was done to the roofs on the buildings," she said, making conversation.

He nodded as he spooned eggs onto his plate. "That storm was a good test for the repairs we made, plus it'll show us if any others are needed."

"Please, God, no more," she murmured under her breath.

"What?"

She waved her fork, dismissing her comment as unimportant.

He looked at her oddly, but she refused to elaborate. He didn't need to know her financial situation. Her money problems were hers and hers alone. Sharing them with him—or anyone, for that matter—was a sure way to have them broadcast all over town.

They ate in silence for a few minutes, and she was sure he wasn't going to pursue the subject any further. To her disappointment he suddenly dropped his fork and braced his hands on his thighs to glare at her.

"I know this is none of my business, but is money tight?"

She busied herself buttering a biscuit. "I don't believe that's any of your business."

"I said as much," he returned in frustration. "But if money's the problem, I can get the glass for you, and you can pay me back when you're able."

"I can afford the glass," she informed him coolly, then lifted a shoulder indifferently. "I just prefer to have it delivered with the other supplies."

"But—"

She held up a hand. "I appreciate your concern, Luke. But I'm the boss, and I'll decide when and if the glass is replaced. Understand?"

He met her gaze for a long moment, then set his jaw and picked up his fork. "Yes, ma'am. I do."

"Lauren!"

Lauren lifted her head at the sound of Rhena's voice. "In the kitchen, Rhena!"

"Luke's truck's at the lodge," Rhena called from the front door, "but he's nowhere in sight. And there's a stray dog out here. It's—get back, dog!" she yelled. "You can't go inside!"

Lauren heard a scuffle, then Buddy raced into the kitchen with Rhena in hot pursuit.

Rhena's eyes widened in surprise when she saw Luke. "What are you doing here?"

He pushed to his feet, looking guilty as hell. "Lauren was kind enough to offer me breakfast, ma'am."

Enjoying his discomfort, Lauren clasped her coffee cup between her hands and smiled at him over the rim. "It was the least I could do, since he stayed the night with me."

Rhena snapped her gaze to Lauren, her shock obvious. "He stayed the night?"

Luke blushed to the roots of his hair. "The storm," he explained. "When I saw it coming, I drove here to spread plastic over the roof. To save the interior, should the roof leak. Got a good soakin' doin' it, and while I was drying off somebody threw a rock through the cabin window. I tried to persuade Lauren to let me drive her to her cousins', but she wouldn't go. I couldn't leave her alone. Not with some vandal on the loose. So I stayed. On the couch," he added quickly.

"Somebody broke a window?" Rhena said in dismay.

Lauren waved away her concern. "We don't know that it was a person. It might have been the wind."

Luke snorted. "It would take a mighty powerful wind to pick up a rock that size and hurl it through a window."

Rhena wrung her hands. "I knew I shouldn't have let Maude talk me into staying in town."

"And what would you have done if you'd been here?" Lauren challenged.

"I don't know," Rhena said in frustration, "but at least you wouldn't have been alone."

Lauren lifted a brow. "I wasn't alone. Remember? Luke was here."

Luke stifled a moan, obviously wishing she hadn't reminded Rhena of his overnight stay.

"You should've let him take you to the Tanners'," Rhena lectured.

"That's the last place I would go," Lauren said bitterly.

"Now that's just plain crazy. The Tanners are family."

Luke cleared his throat, as if to remind the two women of his presence. "Uh, if it's all right, I need to run home and check on a few things. Shouldn't take long."

Lauren scraped back her chair. "Fine," she said to him, then turned on Rhena. "And you know as well as I do that my family lives in Dallas. I have no family here."

On the drive to the Bar-T, Luke debated whether or not he should tell Ry about the incident with the broken window. Duty told him he should, as Ry had, in a sense, hired him to keep an eye on Lauren. But he was working for Lauren, too, so where did his loyalties lie? With Lauren? Or with the Tanner brothers?

As he passed the ranch house, he slowed the truck, telling himself he owed it to Ry to at least tell him about the incident. But then he remembered Lauren saying that the only persons she knew who might want to harm her were the Tanners, and he pressed down the accelerator and drove to the bunkhouse.

He didn't believe for a minute that the Tanner brothers would hurt so much as a hair on her head, but she'd planted the seed of doubt in his mind so strongly that he was beginning to question the Tanners' reasons for asking him to spy on her. Ry had claimed it was because they were worried about her. Said she'd had a rough time of it lately.

Did her rough times have anything to do with money? he wondered.

He dismissed the thought as soon as it arose. Hell, she was a Tanner, and everybody knew the Tanners had more money than God. He supposed he could ask Ry about her financial situation. But if Lauren caught wind of him discussing her affairs with her cousins, he knew there'd be hell to pay. Her dislike for the Tanners ran deep, though why he wasn't sure.

After showering and changing clothes, he headed for town, still puzzling over Lauren's relationship with her cousins. As far as he knew, communication between the two families had ended when Lauren's father had refused to sell Buck the lodge. Luke found it hard to believe the two families hadn't mended their fences at some point over the years. Twenty-five-odd years was a hell of a long time to hold a grudge. But even Buck's death, almost two years before, hadn't put an end to the family feud. Neither Randall nor any of his kin had shown up for Buck's funeral, a slight that had kept tongues wagging in Tanner's Crossing for weeks afterward.

A person would think that Lauren's move to Tanner's Crossing was a sign that she was ready to bury the hatchet. But according to Ry, she had stiff-armed every one of the brothers' attempts at reconciliation, which was why Ry had asked him to keep an eye on her. And that put Luke right smack in the middle between the warring factions. An uncomfortable spot to be, he was beginning to discover.

Noticing the lumberyard ahead, on impulse, he pulled into the loading area.

Jerry, the owner, was outside sliding two-by-fours into a tall bin. Spotting Luke, he stripped off his gloves and headed his way. "Hey, Luke," he called. "What can I do for you today?"

"I believe you're holding an order for Lauren Tanner."

Jerry beamed. "Matter of fact, I am. Got it stacked on a pallet in the shed, marked to deliver next week."

"Just so happens I'm headed there now. If it's all right with you, I'll take it along with me."

Jerry's smile faded. "But I've already figured in delivery charges."

And judging by Jerry's disappointed expression, Luke figured he'd gouged her pretty good with the price.

"Should be easy enough to deduct," Luke replied, with a shrug. "And I'll need a couple of panes of glass," he added. "But bill 'em to me, not her."

Luke drove his truck to the rear of the lodge and climbed down, trying to think of a way to tell Lauren he'd picked up her order that wouldn't make her mad. He'd just begun to unload the supplies, when Rhena stepped out onto the back porch. All the embarrassment he'd experienced that morning washed over him again.

"What's that you've got?" she asked curiously.

"Lauren's order from the lumberyard. I was in town, so I thought I'd go ahead and pick it up. Save Jerry having to drive all the way out here next week."

She nodded, then frowned and moved to the edge of the porch. "If you can spare a minute, I'd like to talk to you."

Luke groaned inwardly, figuring she was going to give him a lecture on propriety and remembering his place. "If it's about last night," he began hesitantly, "it's not like you think. The only reason I stayed at the cabin was to look after Lauren. We didn't…that is to say, I—" He heaved a breath. "Nothing happened," he finished miserably.

"What goes on between you and Lauren is y'all's business, not mine. My only concern is her safety." She folded her arms beneath her breasts and shook her head. "She's stubborn. No one knows that better than me. I was the one who raised her, after all. And knowing how stubborn she can be," she continued, "I'd imagine she kicked up a pretty good fuss when you offered to drive her to the Tanners'."

"Yes, ma'am, she did."

"Well, I just wanted you to know that I appreciate you sticking with her, when she refused to go. I doubt she wanted you staying with her. Prefers to think she can take care of herself."

"I've noticed that about her."

"Nothing wrong with a woman being independent," she told him. "But when Lauren balks, you never know what you're butting up against, her stubbornness or her independence. Makes it hard to keep her out of harm's way."

Since Luke had experienced her stubbornness firsthand, he understood Rhena's concern. But he wasn't sure why she felt the need to tell him all this, or how he was supposed to respond.

"If you're asking me to keep an eye out for her, you have my word. I will."

She gave him a satisfied nod. "Can't ask any more of a man than that."

He hesitated a moment, wanting to ask her about Lauren's relationship with the Tanners, yet unsure if he should. But if the Tanners were truly a threat to her, he needed to know.

"I was a bit surprised when she refused to go to her cousins' place."

"I'm not," she said bluntly. "She doesn't care for them."

"Oh." He couldn't think of anything else to say.

"I was hoping her move here would change things," Rhena said with regret, "but it didn't. I have to give the Tanner brothers credit. They've tried. It's Lauren who won't forgive and forget."

Forget what? was on the tip of his tongue to ask, but Rhena didn't give him a chance to pose the question.

She glanced toward the bed of his truck and frowned. "Is that glass I see in there?"

Luke followed her gaze. "Yes, ma'am. Bought it to fix the broken window."

"I don't recall her calling the lumberyard and ordering glass."

"She didn't. Fact is, she told me that the plastic would do just fine until next week."

"She isn't going to like it when she finds out you've defied her orders," she warned.

"No, ma'am. I doubt she will. But plastic isn't going to keep someone out who wants in. That window needs fixin' and I intend to fix it, whether she likes it or not."

Rhena studied him a moment, then sputtered a laugh as she turned around to enter the lodge. "It'll be interesting to see who wins that little battle."

Yeah, Luke thought, as he began to unload the supplies again. It'll be interesting, all right. A bark had him lifting his head, and he smiled when he saw Buddy running from the woods straight for him.

Hunkering down, Luke scrubbed the dog's head when he reached him. "Hey, Buddy. Have you been keeping an eye on things while I was gone?"

Buddy sank down on his haunches and barked once, as if to report that all was quiet on the Western front.

Chuckling, Luke pushed to his feet and looked around. "Where's Lauren?" he asked.

Buddy took off like a shot for the woods again. Assuming that the dog knew where Lauren was, Luke followed. He found her squatting next to the bank of a creek, a spade in her hand and a bucket of bulbs propped by her feet.

"Need some help?" he asked.

She jumped, then spun on her heels and gave him a

sour look. "You shouldn't sneak up on people like that. You nearly scared the life out of me."

It was all Luke could do not to laugh. With her hair pulled back in a ponytail and mud smearing one cheek, she looked more like a kid making mud pies than a grown woman.

"Sorry. What are you doing?"

Twisting back around, she stabbed her spade into the mud. "Planting bulbs. I wanted to get them in the ground, while it was still soft enough to work."

He hunkered down beside her and took the spade from her hand. "I'll dig," he offered. "You plant."

She swiped the back of a gloved hand over her brow, leaving a streak of mud behind. "Ten inches apart and about six deep," she instructed, as she plucked a bulb from the bucket.

He scooped out one hole and started on the next. "What type of flowers are you planting?"

"Water cannas and spider lilies."

He glanced around, wondering about the location she'd chosen. "Seems a waste to put them here. Wouldn't they be seen and appreciated more closer to the lodge?"

"They'll be seen and appreciated by the guests attending the weddings that'll be held here."

He stopped digging to look at her in confusion. "Weddings? Here? In the woods?"

She poked a bulb into a hole and covered it with mud. "Yes, in the woods." She jerked a thumb over her shoulder, indicating the area behind them, then dropped her hand to pat the mud over the bulb, securing it in place. "I'm going to lay stone over the path and set up chairs on either side of it. The path will lead to a stone patio I'm going to build for the wedding party to stand on, and the creek and the flowers we're planting will serve as a natural backdrop for the ceremony."

Luke glanced over his shoulder at the faint path and the dead grass and leaves that flanked it, and tried to imagine a wedding taking place there. "If you say so," he said doubtfully.

She rolled her eyes. "Men," she muttered. "No imagination." She pointed a stiff finger at the ground. "Just dig."

After the last bulb was planted, Luke gathered up the bucket and spade and followed her back to the lodge. When she jerked to a stop, he had to sidestep to keep from plowing into her.

"What?" he asked in confusion.

"Where did *that* come from?"

He followed the line of her gaze and winced, having forgotten about the supplies he'd unloaded. "I was in town. Figured I'd pick up your supplies and save Jerry having to make the delivery."

Seeing the anger building on her face, he pulled the invoice from his pocket. "I made sure he deducted the delivery charge."

"I didn't ask you to pick up my supplies."

"No," he agreed. "Just made sense to do it, since I was already in town."

Setting her jaw, she marched to his truck to inspect her order. Her jaw tightened even more when she saw the glass.

"You have no right to charge items to my account," she said tersely.

"I didn't. I charged it to mine."

His explanation didn't calm her. If anything, it incensed her more.

She thrust out a hand. "I want the invoice."

He pulled it from his pocket and laid it on her palm. She curled her fingers around it, wadding it in her fist.

"No one decides how or when my money is spent but me. Understand?"

"Yes, ma'am. I do."

"You'll receive a reimbursement with your next paycheck, but don't you *ever* do anything like this again." Having had her say, she spun on her heel and stalked away.

Luke stared after her, wondering what he'd done that was so wrong.

"Stubbornness or independence?"

He whirled to find Rhena standing on the porch, obviously having witnessed the exchange. Grimacing, he lifted a shoulder. "Doesn't matter. Mad is mad in my book, and she's plenty mad at me."

"Don't let her anger bother you," she said kindly. "What you did was a nice thing. She'll realize that, once she cools off. You'll see."

Luke wondered how long it was going to take for Lauren to cool off. She hadn't spoken to him in the three days since she'd given him the tongue-lashing. When he arrived at the lodge for work each morning, he'd find a note tacked to the back porch with a list of jobs for him to complete that day. He didn't know what

Lauren did while he was working, but whatever it was, it kept her out of sight and away from him.

That she was angry with him bothered him like nothing had ever bothered him before. He'd known he was overstepping his bounds when he picked up her order at the lumberyard. And he'd known he was defying her explicit instructions when he bought and paid for the glass. But he'd never expected her to react the way she had.

But after three days of her particular form of punishment, Luke quit being bothered and got downright mad himself. It wasn't like he'd done anything to purposefully hurt her, he told himself as he chopped firewood, the last chore on the list she'd left for him that day. She was the one who'd placed the order for the supplies, not him. He'd simply saved her the cost of delivery, a favor she should be grateful for, not resent. And so what if he'd purchased a couple of pieces of glass to replace her damn window? The cost was less than twenty bucks. Big deal. He sure as hell hadn't expected her to pay him back, nor had he asked her to.

Taking another log from the stack to be split, he upended it on the old tree stump, lifted the ax above his head and brought it down, splitting the log in two.

It was backbreaking work, and a job she'd added to the list just to be ornery, he was sure, since he'd already split at least two cords of wood over the last few days. Muttering curses under his breath, he picked up the split wood, placed it in the rack, then pulled another log from the dwindling pile.

He'd just lifted the ax above his head when Buddy, who'd been napping under the truck, emitted a low growl, then took off like a shot for the woods. Frowning, Luke lowered the ax and watched him. Had he seen a squirrel? he wondered. Or picked up the scent of another animal?

With a shrug, he lifted the ax again…and lowered it just as quickly when another possibility came to mind. *Lauren.* For all Luke knew, she could be in the woods right now and in some kind of trouble. Dropping the ax, he grabbed his shotgun from the tailgate of the truck and ran after Buddy, following the sound of the dog's barking. Once under the cover of the woods, he leaped over fallen limbs, darted around trees blocking his way and slapped at vines that wrapped themselves around him trying to slow him down.

As he ran, he told himself that he was probably overreacting, that Lauren was probably safe in the lodge right now, painting doors or polishing floors, and Buddy was probably just on a hunt. But something kept pushing him onward, his chest growing tighter and tighter with each step that took him deeper into the woods. Out of breath, he stopped for a moment and listened for Buddy's bark. The tone of it had changed, he realized. Shriller now, more frantic. He plunged on, crashing through the undergrowth, calling her name. "Lauren! Lauren, where are you?"

He stopped again to listen, and was sure he heard a voice.

"Lauren!" he shouted, and started running again. "Lauren, answer me!"

"Here."

Her voice was small, barely audible over the thundering of his heart. He ran toward the sound, crashing through the underbrush, and found her sitting on the ground, hunched over, holding her head between her hands. Leaves and dead vegetation clung to the back of her shirt and tangled in her hair. Buddy was with her, licking her face. As soon as Luke dropped to a knee beside them, Buddy took off again, barking furiously.

Luke placed a hand gently on her back. "Are you hurt?"

She drew in a ragged breath. "I don't think so. I fell. Hit my head."

He crouched in front of her and forced up her chin. Though her face was dirty and scratched, he didn't see any bruises or lumps. "Where?" he asked.

She laid a hand tentatively on the back of her head and winced. "Here." She drew her hand away and Luke saw the blood smeared on her fingers.

He set his jaw. "We need to get you back to the lodge."

"Okay." She tried to stand, but her legs wouldn't support her. "Give me a minute," she said weakly.

Luke scooped her up into his arms. "I'll carry you."

He retraced his steps through the woods, his return much slower. Since Lauren's cabin was closer than the lodge, he carried her inside and deposited her on the sofa.

"I'll get a cloth and some water," he told her, then hurried to the bathroom.

When he returned, she was slumped on the sofa, her head resting on its back.

"Lauren?"

She blinked open her eyes to peer at him, then closed them again. "Dizzy," she murmured.

He sank down beside her. "Turn onto your side," he instructed, "so I can see the wound."

She rolled to her hip, turning her back to him. Being as gentle as possible, he parted her hair and examined her scalp as he dabbed away the blood and dirt.

"You've got a lump the size of an egg," he told her, "but the cut is small and not very deep."

The front door opened and Rhena burst in, her face creased with worry. "What happened?"

"Nothing," Lauren said weakly. "I tripped over a log and fell."

Rhena looked at Luke, as if asking him to confirm the story. When he only lifted a shoulder, she plopped down on the sofa in front of Lauren. "How many times have I told you not to go out alone?" she scolded. "What if Luke hadn't found you? You could've died in those woods, and nobody would've been the wiser."

Lauren pressed her hands over her ears. "Please," she begged. "No lectures. Not now."

Though it was obvious Rhena would've liked to say more, she released a long breath. "What you need is a good warm soak in the tub. Come on," she said and helped Lauren to her feet. "You'll feel better after you're all cleaned up."

At the bedroom door, Lauren stopped. "Buddy," she said, and glanced over her shoulder at Luke. "Where's Buddy?

Luke picked up his hat. "Don't worry. I'll find him."

Once outside, Luke headed straight for the woods. He intended to find Buddy, as he'd promised, but first he wanted another look at the place where Lauren had fallen. She'd claimed a log was the cause of her fall, but he wasn't so sure.

He found the location easily enough and hunkered down to examine the ground more closely, noting the direction of her footprints, the crushed vegetation that marked her fall. The log she said she'd tripped over was there, just as she'd claimed. But something didn't feel right to Luke. Lauren wasn't a clumsy woman, nor was she careless. Granted, the log was half-rotted and buried beneath a tangle of vines, but he couldn't imagine her not seeing it. Besides, if the log had tripped her, the damage would've been to the front of her face, not the back of her head.

Pushing his hands against his thighs, he rose and looked around. A branch, three or more inches thick, lay to the left of the spot where Lauren had fallen. Though the branch was obviously dead, upon closer inspection, Luke discovered the severed end looked like a fresh break. Turning the branch slowly, he spotted several black hairs clinging to the bark.

He looked up into the canopy of branches overhead and scanned the tree's trunk until he found the jagged cut where the limb had once been attached to the tree. Since the limb was dead and had been for some time, it was reasonable to assume that the limb's fall was caused by nature.

But Luke wasn't ready to rule Lauren's accident as simply a matter of her being at the wrong place at the wrong time.

He circled the tree, smoothing a hand over its rough bark. Finding a pattern of chips in the bark, he stopped and frowned. Something—or some*one*—had recently climbed the tree. It wasn't a stretch to imagine that whoever had climbed it had caused the limb to fall on Lauren. The canopy of leaves in the live oak provided a perfect cover until just the right moment. A little pressure asserted on the dead limb and it would've snapped off and crashed to the ground, striking Lauren on the head. If it had fallen a split second sooner, the limb would've hit her square on top of her head and the outcome would've been entirely different…possibly deadly.

Hearing a crashing sound in the brush behind him, Luke lifted his shotgun and whirled, expecting to confront Lauren's attacker. When it was Buddy who appeared from the brush, he lowered the gun and sank to a knee.

"Hey, Buddy," he said, giving the dog a brisk rub. "Did you catch the person who attacked Lauren?"

The dog laid its head on Luke's thigh and whined sorrowfully, as if ashamed that he'd returned empty-handed.

"Don't worry," Luke assured him, as he rose. "Whoever did this isn't going to hurt her again. Not if I have a say in the matter."

"I'm not going anywhere," Lauren said stubbornly.

"Now, Lauren," Rhena began.

"No!" Lauren snapped. "I refuse to let anyone frighten me away from my own home."

"Then at least move up to the lodge with Miss Rhena," Luke suggested patiently.

She folded her arms across her chest. "No. Whoever

is responsible for this is obviously targeting me. If I move to the lodge, then I'd be putting Rhena in danger."

When Rhena would've argued, Luke held up a hand. "No. Lauren's right. Both attacks have been aimed directly at her. If someone had wanted to hurt you, Miss Rhena, they could've done so any number of times."

"My point exactly," Lauren said smugly.

Seated on the hearth, Luke studied the toes of his boots, trying to think who would want to hurt Lauren. Unable to come up with anyone, he lifted his head to peer at her. "Do you have any enemies in the area?"

She rolled her eyes. "As I've told you before, I haven't lived here long enough to make any enemies."

"What about your ex-husband?"

She choked a laugh. "All Devon wanted from me was my money and he's already gotten all of that."

He glanced at Rhena, silently asking her opinion.

She lifted a shoulder. "Devon wouldn't do something like this. He's too lazy."

Scowling, Lauren broke off a piece of her cookie and fed it to Buddy. "If you're looking for someone to pin the blame on, look at the Tanners."

Luke shook his head. "I know the Tanner brothers. They'd never lay a hand on a woman."

"Maybe not," Lauren conceded. "But that doesn't mean they wouldn't pay someone to do their dirty work for them."

Frustrated, Luke stood. "What is it with you and the Tanners? What did they do to you to make you hate them so much?"

"Not to me. My family."

He waited for her to say more. When she didn't, he heaved a sigh and sat back down on the hearth. "Maybe you should call the sheriff. Tell him your suspicions."

She looked at him in amazement. "Are you kidding? The Tanners *own* this town."

"You're a Tanner, too," he reminded her.

"Not from *that* branch of Tanners. My father left Tanner's Crossing to escape the power Buck wielded over him and everybody else in this town. I won't let his sons intimidate me into leaving, too."

"I know the Tanners," he said, struggling for patience. "They wouldn't harm a fly."

"Maybe not personally," she replied. "Like I said, they wouldn't think twice about paying someone to do their dirty work for them. They can certainly afford it."

Before he could think of an argument to offer, she flapped a hand, as if dismissing the subject. "It doesn't matter who's responsible. I'm not going to let anyone scare me away. This is my home now, and I intend to stay."

Luke dropped his face to his hands and scrubbed, trying to think of a way to persuade her to leave. Unable to come up with one, he dragged his hands from his face and braced them on his thighs. "Then I'm staying, too."

Her eyes widened. "Here?"

He nodded. "I can bunk on the sofa, same as I did the other night."

"No! I won't let—"

"Yes, you will," Rhena ordered, cutting her off. "If you don't, then I'm calling your daddy and telling him what's going on here."

She gave Rhena a murderous look. "I don't want my

father dragged into this. He's suffered enough because of the Tanners."

Rhena opened her hands. "The choice is yours. Either Luke stays or I'm calling your daddy."

Lauren glared at Rhena a full minute, then turned to Luke. "Fine," she snapped, her resentment obvious. "You can stay." She pushed from the sofa and stalked to her bedroom. In the doorway she stopped and glanced back, burning them both with a look. "But I want you to know that this is the last time I'll allow either of you to use my father to blackmail me."

Before either could reply, she slammed the door, shutting them out.

Five

Luke had never lived with a woman before. Not that he considered sleeping on Lauren's sofa for a week the same as living with her. Theirs was strictly a temporary arrangement and definitely not based on romance. She resented his presence and wasn't hesitant about letting him know how she felt.

For his part, he did his best to stay out of her way. He rose before she did each morning and hightailed it for the lodge, where he ate breakfast with Rhena. In the afternoons he drove to the Bar-T, completed his chores as quickly as possible, then drove back to the lodge. He worked outside as long as the light held, had dinner with Rhena in the kitchen of the lodge, showered, then headed back to the cabin. Lauren had an uncanny sense of anticipating his arrival and was usually locked in her bedroom by the time he entered the cabin.

Considering her surly attitude toward him and the small amount of time they actually breathed the same air, Luke found it amazing that he'd developed what could only be called a crush on the woman. He found himself constantly thinking about her. And when he wasn't thinking about her, he was looking for an excuse to seek her out.

At night he lay awake long after he'd turned out the light, listening for any sounds that came from her bedroom. Through his nocturnal study, he'd discovered some of her habits and established her bedtime routine. She preferred a shower to a bath, brushed her teeth for a full two minutes and slept in a fancy silk nightgown that touched her bare toes. He'd discovered the latter late one night, when Buddy insisted upon being let outside, long after Luke had gone to bed. Since there was only one door into the cabin, Lauren was forced to pass by the sofa on her way to let the dog out. Luke had pretended to be asleep, but he'd stolen a peek as she stood waiting by the door for Buddy's return. Though he'd never admit to the deception, he had paid dearly for his voyeurism.

The nightgown she'd worn wasn't sheer, but it was damn close, revealing soft curves and shadowed breasts beneath. Thanks to Buddy and the call of nature, he now had more vivid images to feed his imagination and keep him awake at night. Images of her lying on her bed, her face relaxed in sleep. Images of him lying beside her. He envisioned himself removing the gown and imagined how the silk would feel on his fingers as he pulled it over her head, how her skin would warm beneath his palms as he swept his hands down her body.

As a result, nighttime had become his enemy, sleep impossible to find. He tossed and turned on the narrow sofa, trying to block the images from his mind, but it was hopeless. Each morning, he rolled off the sofa before Lauren arose, as weary as when he'd first lain down. The dark circles that shadowed his eyes made him look like a raccoon, and the lack of sleep was beginning to take its toll. Twice he'd dozed off while Rhena was cooking his breakfast. Once he'd even fallen asleep behind the wheel of his truck. If not for the blare of the horn from an oncoming car startling him awake, he might've hit the vehicle head-on.

To make matters worse, his conscience was giving him fits. He knew he should have told Ry about the trouble Lauren was having at the lodge, but every time he saw Ry, he let the opportunity pass without addressing the subject. He supposed it was his loyalty to Lauren that kept him quiet. It sure as hell wasn't because he thought the Tanner brothers were behind the trouble she was having.

They wouldn't think twice about paying someone to do their dirty work for them.

Her accusation replayed in his mind as he drove by Ry's house. He slowed the truck, frowning at the house as he gave that possibility more thought. If Buck were alive, Luke didn't doubt for a minute that the elder Tanner would be the one responsible for trying to run Lauren off. Intimidation was Buck's specialty. And when intimidation didn't work, he hired goons to do the convincing for him.

Had his sons inherited their father's penchant for power, his vindictive streak? Luke wondered. He'd never seen evidence of either trait in any of the Tanner brothers…but just because he'd never witnessed them, didn't mean they didn't exist.

His frown deepening, he pressed on the accelerator and drove on past the ranch house and to the barn where his chores awaited him, his thoughts troubled, his eyes burning from lack of sleep.

While Luke was contemplating his chores at the Bar-T, Lauren and Rhena were busy scrubbing the interior windows at the lodge.

"I'm worried about Luke," Rhena said,

Lauren rolled her eyes, then attacked the dirt and grime on the window again. "Who *don't* you worry about?"

Rhena gave her a sour look, before dipping her rag in the cleaning solvent. "He doesn't look well to me," Rhena said, as she wrung out her rag. "Do you suppose he could be suffering some kind of complications from his burns?"

"How the heck would I know?" Lauren asked impatiently. "The man doesn't speak more than three words a day."

"Maybe not to you," Rhena said smugly. "But he talks to me."

Lauren looked at Rhena in surprise, then scowled and resumed her scrubbing. "If y'all are so chummy, why don't you ask him if something is wrong?"

"No. He's self-conscious enough about his appearance. If I let on I thought he looked sick, it would only make things worse. No," she said again. "I wouldn't do that to him. He's much too kind for me to take a chance on offending him."

Her scowl deepening, Lauren picked up the bucket from the floor and moved down to the next set of windows. "Honestly, Rhena. You'd think the man was God or something, the way you fuss over him. Cooking his meals and doing his laundry. With the amount of time he spends at the lodge, I don't know why he doesn't simply move in with you."

"Jealous?"

Lauren dropped her hand and stared. "Jealous?" she repeated, then sputtered a laugh and slapped her rag against the window and scrubbed furiously. "Yeah, like I'd be jealous over Luke."

"I've seen the way you look at him, when you think no one is watching. Like you'd like nothing better than to strip him naked."

"Rhena!" Lauren cried, aghast. "I do not!"

Her smile smug, Rhena swiped away a streak of dirt Lauren had missed. "No sense trying to deny it. I may be old, but I'm not blind." She cast a sideways glance at Lauren. "And he looks at you the same way."

Lauren tensed at the news, but refused to meet Rhena's gaze. "You're making that up."

"It's the God's truth. The man is smitten. He can hardly keep his eyes off you."

Squatting beside the bucket, Lauren wrung out her rag. "Now I know you're lying."

"You think so?" Rhena challenged. "Then tell me

why he insists on staying out here and looking after you, when he could just as easily go home and sleep in his own bed?"

"I don't know," Lauren said, dismissing the suggestion with a shrug. "He's probably from the old school. Considers it his manly duty to protect a member of the weaker sex."

"Uh-huh," Rhena said doubtfully.

"You've seen how he is," Lauren said defensively. "Stands until we're seated. 'Yes ma'ams' and 'no ma'ams' us to death. Insists upon opening doors for us."

"And what's wrong with that?"

"Did I say there was anything wrong with it?" Lauren cried, then groaned, when Rhena merely smiled. Lauren threw down her rag and marched for the door. "I need some air," she muttered.

"What you need," Rhena called after her, "is to rip off Luke's shirt and see what's underneath. Who knows? You might like what you find."

Lauren set her teeth, but kept walking, refusing to give Rhena the satisfaction of a response.

Two days later Luke sat on the examining table in Ry's office, pulling his shirt back on, while Ry scribbled notations on his chart.

"We can schedule the surgery for next week," Ry said, flipping a page.

Luke's fingers froze on the button he was closing. "Next week?" he repeated.

Ry glanced up from his swivel chair. "Yeah. Is that a problem?"

Avoiding Ry's gaze, Luke slid off the table and tucked his shirt into the waist of his jeans. "Well, yeah. I need to be at the lodge."

Ry laid down his pen, his forehead creased in concern. "I've noticed you haven't been coming home at night. Everything's all right over there, isn't it?"

It was the perfect opening for Luke to tell Ry about the broken window and Lauren's accident, and watch his reaction for any signs of guilt.

Instead he heard himself saying, "Everything's fine. It's just that there's still a lot of work to be done and she's got hunters coming in less than two weeks. Staying at the lodge saves me driving time and gives me a chance to get more done."

"Timing is crucial in performing the surgeries," Ry reminded him. "It's taken us a year to get this far. The longer we wait, the more scar tissue will build up and the greater the risk of nerve damage and complications."

Luke ducked his head and nodded. "Yeah. I know."

"Surely she can spare you for a couple of days. A week at the most."

"I don't know, Ry," he said doubtfully.

Ry stood and clapped a hand on his shoulder. "Look, Luke, I know that we dumped this on you, and I admire you for wanting to help our cousin out and see the project to its end. But you've got to think of yourself. Delaying the surgery could severely lessen the success of the operation."

"I know," Luke said miserably.

Ry gave his shoulder a reassuring squeeze. "Think about it. Discuss it with Lauren, if you feel you need to.

But I'm going to go ahead and put you on the schedule for first thing Monday morning. If I don't do it now, there's a chance the slots will fill up and we won't be able to get you in."

Luke nodded soberly, aware of the risk he was taking, if he put off the surgery. "All right. I'll let you know."

Luke worked until almost dark, debating how best to approach Lauren about needing some time off. Simply telling her outright about his surgery didn't sit well with him. He considered any kind of sickness a weakness, and feared she'd think the same. And he didn't want her to think any less of him than she already did. Why he cared what she thought, he wasn't sure, since there wasn't a chance in hell of them ever having a relationship other than that of boss to employee. Still, a man had his pride.

He waited until he saw her head for the cabin, then started after her.

"Lauren!" he called. "Wait up. I need to talk to you a minute."

She stopped and turned. "What about?"

He pulled off his hat and turned it nervously between his hands. "I was wonderin' if you'd mind if I took some time off next week?"

Her eyes widened in alarm. "But we've got less than two weeks to get ready for the hunters!"

He ducked his head and nodded. "I know. But I've got some business to tend to."

"Can't it wait? You know how important it is for me to be ready."

"Yes, ma'am, I do," he agreed, then heaved a sigh and settled his hat back over his head. "Don't worry. I'll see the job to the end."

As Lauren lay in bed that night, she felt small, mean and selfish. Not once in the two weeks Luke had worked for her had he asked for a day off. And to think of all the extra things he'd done for her without accepting any compensation in return! Driving to the lodge in a thunderstorm to spread plastic over the roofs of her buildings. Buying the glass and replacing the window that was broken. Insisting on picking up supplies in town in order to save her the delivery charges. He'd even slept on her sofa for a week in order to protect her.

And she'd refused the one favor he'd asked of her.

But she needed his help, she argued silently. This last week of preparation was crucial to her business's success, and there was still so much to be done. He knew how important her plans for this place were to her. Or at least he should. She'd certainly told him often enough.

Groaning her frustration, she rolled to her side and punched up her pillow beneath her cheek. Why would he ask off, when he knew how much she needed him? Why would he put her in such an awkward position, knowing that she couldn't do the work alone?

She wanted to believe that his request was because he was thoughtless, uncaring. That he'd purposely staged this sudden need to be elsewhere just so that she would fail.

But she knew that wasn't true. Luke wasn't like that.

He was a nice man, a kind man. He'd been nothing but honest with her from the first. And he was generous to a fault, with the time and sweat he'd put into helping her get the lodge ready for guests.

And she was a first-class bitch.

Regretting her less-than-altruistic response to a man who had given so unselfishly, she slowly climbed from her bed and pulled on her robe. "Stay," she whispered to Buddy, when he lifted his head. With a sigh, the dog lay back down and closed his eyes.

She opened the bedroom door a crack and peeked out into the den. A beam of moonlight slanting through the window offered the only illumination. Luke lay on the sofa, his head propped up on one end, his feet hanging over the other. The blanket she'd provided draped his midsection and hung off the side of the sofa, leaving his chest and legs exposed. Hot natured? she wondered. Or had he kicked off the covering, because he was uncomfortable?

Feeling a twinge of guilt for not having offered him her own bed, she tiptoed across the room to peer down at him. His eyes were closed and his breathing rhythmic, letting her know that he was asleep. He looked so peaceful, she really hated to wake him.

Realizing the rareness of this opportunity to study him unaware, she leaned closer. Though he no longer tried to hide his face from her, she avoided looking at him directly or too intently, fearing he'd think she was staring at his scars and would become self-conscious again. His scars were nothing to be embarrassed about, and she wondered if it was the memory of his appearance prior to the surgeries on his face that haunted him still.

She let her gaze slide farther down, over his chin and to his chest, and pressed her fingers to her mouth to smother a low moan. The scar that she'd glimpsed briefly before was definitely much worse than those on his face. Without thinking, she touched a finger to the puckered flesh.

A hand clamped her wrist, and she swallowed a scream, as Luke sat bolt upright, his eyes wide.

His fingers dug into her flesh as he stared at her, slowly bringing her into focus. His chest heaving, he loosened his grip. "What the hell are you doing?"

She gulped, swallowed, her eyes locked on his. "N-nothing. I…I just wanted to tell you that you could take time off next week."

He blew out a long breath and sank back against the sofa, his eyes shuttering closed. "Why?" he asked in a hoarse voice, then amended his question to, "What made you change your mind?"

She dropped her gaze, ashamed of her prior behavior. "I was thinking only of myself. You've been nothing but kind to me, and I returned that kindness with selfishness. I…I'm sorry," she finished feebly. She lifted her gaze and found his eyes on her. "I really am," she said, and meant it. "Take whatever time you need. Rhena and I will manage."

He closed his eyes again on a sigh, seeming relieved that she'd given him her permission. "I'll double my hours between now and Monday," he promised. "I'll get as much done as I can before I have to leave."

She felt a moment's panic, wondering if he meant to

go away for good. She tried her best to hide her fear from him. "You are coming back, aren't you?"

He opened his eyes and met her gaze. "You can bet on it."

She nearly wilted at the warmth in his brown eyes, the tenderness in his smile. Feeling as if her knees were going to fold, she sank onto the edge of the sofa beside him. She wanted to say so much to him, avoid ending this moment.

"I really appreciate all you've done for me," she began hesitantly, then dropped her gaze, remembering all the times she'd yelled at him and been rude to him. "I know that you've put up with a lot of grief from me."

His chuckle drew her gaze back to his and she was surprised to see the teasing that twinkled in his eyes.

"I've suffered worse."

She returned his smile, relieved that he didn't seem to hold her ungracious behavior against her.

"I can't imagine from whom. I can be a bitch sometimes. I know. Rhena accuses me of it often enough."

He folded one arm behind his head, looking more relaxed and at ease than she had ever seen him.

"You've got a good friend in Miss Rhena."

"No one is more aware of that than me. I don't know what I'd do without her."

"You'd do just fine. You're stronger than you think."

She looked at him curiously. "That's odd that you would say that. Rhena said almost exactly that same thing to me."

He winked at her. "Like minds. She's what my mama would call good folks."

Her smile faded, as she thought of the danger she had unwittingly placed Rhena in by allowing her to come to Tanner's Crossing with her. "I don't want her hurt because of her loyalty to me."

He took her hand and gave it a squeeze. "Nobody's gonna get hurt. I'll see to that."

She lifted a brow. "And who's going to protect us while our self-proclaimed bodyguard is away?"

When she saw his stricken look, she quickly shook her head. "Forget I said that. It was just a joke."

"Why don't you go to your—"

She pressed a finger against his lips, silencing him before he could finish. "No. I'm staying right here."

Scowling, he plucked her hand from his mouth. "You've got to be the stubbornest woman I've ever met."

Not wanting to discuss her relationship with her cousins again, she teased, "Is there a prize to go with that title?"

With a sigh, he drew her hand to hold against his chest. "I wish you'd tell me why you dislike them so much."

Though he seemed unaware of their joined hands or where he'd placed them, her insides quivered with awareness. "Past history," she said, then forced a smile. "Now about that prize…"

He choked a laugh. "If there was one, you'd win it."

"I've always strived to be the best at everything I do."

"I don't doubt that for a minute."

Unable to think of anything more to say, she dropped her gaze. It settled on the scar on his chest.

"Does it bother you?" she asked hesitantly, then quickly shifted her gaze to his, fearing he'd misunderstand her question. "I mean, does it ever hurt?"

His smile softened, as if to ease her concern. "Not enough to complain about. The healing process was the worst. The burns had to scab over, then be scraped. There were times I wished I'd died in the fire."

Her eyes widened in horror. "You don't mean that!"

"I don't now, but I did then. The pain was…there aren't words to describe it. It was hell. But I couldn't give up. There's always a reason to live."

Unable to imagine that kind of suffering, she grew pensive. "How long were you in the hospital?"

"Months. First in Dallas at the Parkland Burn Center. Then I was moved to the hospital here in Tanner's Crossing."

Remembering what he'd told her about his family, she said, "And you had no one to stay with you, be with you."

"Even if I had, there was nothing anyone could've done. The medical staff took good care of me." He chuckled, the sound vibrating against the hand he still held against his chest. "Though I'm sure they were glad to see my backside the day I left. I wasn't always the model patient. I gave 'em hell during most of the treatments."

"And who would blame you?" she said indignantly. "The pain must've been horrible."

"And then some," he said dryly, then shrugged. "But there were folks there who had it worse than me. Made me feel like a baby for complaining."

Thoughtful, Lauren studied the scar. "Where all were you burned?"

"Face, back, chest. They caught the worst of it. My hands were burned, too." He lifted his free one for her to see. "They looked worse before the surgeries. If not for Ry, I might've lost some of my fingers."

Though grateful that Ry Tanner had given Luke the care he needed, Lauren refused to so much as voice her cousin's name out loud, much less give him the credit he obviously deserved.

Instead she focused on Luke's hand. "That's why you wear gloves all the time, isn't it? To hide your hands."

He curled his fingers against his palm, as if only now aware his hand was exposed. "Yeah. No sense making folks look at 'em when I can just as easily keep them from sight."

Her heart melting, she took his hand and pried his fingers open. "There's nothing wrong with your hands, Luke," she said softly.

He snorted. "Nothing but the fact that they're big and ugly. Half the time I don't know what to do with 'em."

She lifted his hand and pressed a kiss to the back of his fingers. "Don't ever say that," she scolded softly. "Your hands are beautiful. Gifted. Think of all the things you do with them. All the good you perform. If not for you and your hands, Buddy wouldn't be alive. And what about all the things you've done around here? You can repair just about anything. I've never known a man with so many skills." She leaned closer, their faces inches apart, and gave him a stern look. "So don't let me ever hear you say your hands are big and ugly."

Smiling, she straightened and laid his hand on his chest. "And I've kept you awake way too long." She rose, then paused, looking down at him. "Thanks, Luke," she said quietly. "For everything."

* * *

Luke watched her cross back to her room and close the door behind her, then lifted the hand she'd kissed to stare at it. The lump in his throat grew until he was sure it would choke him. She'd kissed his hand. His big, ugly hand, with its gnarled fingers, oversize knuckles and puckered flesh. No one had ever done anything like that before. Not even before the fire.

He covered his left hand with his right, as if to hold the kiss there, then lifted his head to stare at her bedroom door. Tears burned behind his eyes.

She'd kissed his hand, he thought again. And she'd said his hands were beautiful. Even gifted. Looking right square at them, she'd claimed they were beautiful and gifted. Either the woman was blind as a bat or she'd been lying through her teeth. There was no other explanation Luke could think of that would make her say such an outrageous thing.

And she'd thanked him. Sincerely thanked him, as if she were truly grateful for all the things he'd done for her.

But it was the kiss that astounded him the most.

Drawing his hand to hold against his chest, he closed his eyes. He was going to remember that kiss, he promised himself. The moist feel of her lips. The featherlight brush of them over his skin. The warmth.

And he was going to try real hard not to imagine what those lips would feel like pressed against his own.

On Monday afternoon Lauren sat at the kitchen table in the lodge, frowning over the sketches of the outdoor wedding chapel she had spread before her. It was a good start, she told herself. Something to build from.

A knock on the screen door had her whipping her head around to stare. A man stood on the other side. A stranger.

"Howdy, ma'am," the man said brightly.

She glanced at the latch on the screen door, and silently cursed herself for not hooking it when she'd come inside.

"You really should keep the door latched," he said, as if reading her mind. "Never know who might show up at your door way out here in the country."

She snapped her gaze to his, then looked beyond him, praying Buddy was close enough so that if she screamed, he'd come running.

"If you're lookin' for your dog," he said, "he's out sniffin' the tires on my truck. Probably'll mark 'em 'fore I leave. Dogs do that, you know. Mark their territory, that is."

She stared at the man incredulously. "Who are you?"

He whipped off his hat and entered the kitchen. "Sorry, ma'am, for not introducin' myself right off. The name's Monty. I'm a friend of Luke's."

Rhena appeared in the doorway, struggling beneath the weight of the canister vacuum.

Monty rushed to take the appliance from her. "Here. Let me get that for you, ma'am."

Rhena drew back to look at him but kept a hand on her vacuum, as if afraid he planned to steal it. "Who are you?"

He beamed. "Monty. I'm a friend of Luke's. He asked me to stop in and check on you ladies."

Rhena released her hold on the vacuum, as if the mention of Luke's name was all the ID she needed. "He's such a thoughtful man. We sure do miss him around here."

"I 'magine he's missin' you ladies, too," Monty replied, then sniffed the air. "Is that corn bread I smell bakin'?"

Rhena bustled to the stove, reminded of her baking. "Yes, if it hasn't burned." She pulled the pan from the oven and sighed, obviously relieved to find that it hadn't. She glanced toward Monty, as she set the pan on the counter. "Would you like to stay and have dinner with us?"

He set the vacuum down and wet his lips. "Why, thank you, ma'am. I'd like that just fine. It isn't often an old, single man like me gets offered a home-cooked meal."

"You're not old," Rhena scolded, then cast him a shy smile. "I'll bet you're not a day over fifty."

Lauren rolled her eyes and gathered her sketches, unable to believe that Rhena would fall for a line like that. "I'm going to the cabin and get my boots. Sounds as if I'm going to need them."

On Wednesday afternoon, Lauren took a much-needed break from cleaning the paneled walls of the lodge's main room and headed for town with Rhena's grocery list tucked into her pocket.

As she pushed the cart down the aisles, mindlessly dumping items into the basket, she mentally reviewed the work still needed to be done on the lodge prior to the arrival of the first group of hunters.

The grounds were as ready as they were going to get, but the lodge itself still needed attention. She would finish cleaning and oiling the paneling before she quit for the night. She had to. The furniture she'd ordered was scheduled for delivery the next day. Rhena had promised to have the linens for the beds ready in the morning, so the beds would have to be made. The bathrooms—all five of the suckers—had been scrubbed and readied for guests. Thankfully, she could mark that unpleasant task off her list. She'd put the last coat of paint on the outdoor furniture the night before. It was just a matter now of setting it out.

She stopped, suddenly realizing that she was going to make her deadline. A week ago, she hadn't thought it possible. She'd been convinced that there was no way she'd have the place ready in time. There had been simply too much to do and too little time left to do it. But thanks to Luke and the long hours he'd put in over the weekend, the bulk of the work was complete.

Luke. What would she have done without him?

She'd be running around like a wild woman, that's what, she told herself as she nabbed a carton of soft drinks and headed for the counter.

Maude lifted a brow in surprise. "Well, hello, stranger. Haven't seen you in here in a month of Sundays."

Lauren sagged her shoulders wearily. "I've been busy. Our hunters are due to arrive the first of next week."

Maude began ringing up the items that Lauren fished from the cart. "Rhena mentioned that the last time she was in. Said she was worried y'all were going to have to pitch tents for them to sleep in."

"So was I," Lauren admitted. "But we're down to the finishing touches now, so we should be ready in time."

"Heard Luke Jordan was working for you."

As owner of the grocery store, Maude knew everyone in town and their activities, so Lauren wasn't surprised that she knew about Luke.

"Yes, and I don't know what we would've done without him. He was a godsend, that's for sure."

Maude shook her head sadly. "Terrible what that fire did to him. And to such a nice man, too."

"He is nice," Lauren agreed.

"Ry's wife, Kayla, was in this morning. Said Luke might get to go home tomorrow."

"Home?" Lauren repeated dully, not knowing what Maude was talking about.

"From the hospital," Maude said, then shook her head again, as she entered the last item into the register. "Amazing, isn't it, what doctors can do these days? Imagine taking a piece of skin from one part of the body and grafting it onto another."

Lauren paled, realizing why Luke had needed time off. He was having more surgery done. And he hadn't even told her!

Maude punched the total key. "That'll be $67.26. Cash or charge?"

Lauren began frantically stuffing the sacks of groceries into the cart. "Put it on my account," she said as she wheeled the cart for the door, then tossed a belated "Thanks, Maude" over her shoulder and all but ran for her car.

Six

Lauren had never cared for hospitals. The antiseptic smell that permeated the air. The bustle of medical personnel up and down the halls. The worried and sometimes hopeless expressions on the faces of the people crowded into the waiting rooms. The confusing maze of hallways and cubicles.

By the time she reached the room number the volunteer manning the information desk had provided, her heart was beating erratically and her stomach was queasy. She placed a hand against the door and drew in a deep, calming breath, before opening it a fraction.

A male voice drifted out.

"You're going to need care once you go home. Bandages changed. Wounds cleaned. That type of thing."

She peeked inside and saw that the voice belonged

to none other than Ry Tanner. Curling her lip in disgust, she started to close the door, thinking she'd come back to see Luke after Ry was gone. But Ry's next words stopped her cold.

"It would probably be best if you stayed at the house with us."

"That's not necessary," she heard Luke say. "Monty can do what needs to be done."

Monty? Lauren thought in dismay. The man was pleasant enough, but she couldn't imagine him performing the kind of duties for Luke that Ry had described.

She heard Ry laugh, and forced herself to listen.

"Monty's good at a lot of things," Ry said, "but nursing isn't one of them. You're better off staying at the house with us."

"I can't do that," Luke argued. "Y'all've already done too much for me."

Lauren set her jaw. Though she felt the Tanners owed Luke a great deal more than a couple of days recuperation at their home, she wasn't about to let Luke obligate himself to them any more than he already had.

Pasting on a smile, she shoved open the door and breezed into the room. "I heard they were cutting you loose today," she said to Luke.

Obviously shocked to see her, he drew the sheet up to his chin. "Uh. Yes, ma'am. Ry and I were just discussing that."

Ignoring Ry, she kept her gaze on Luke and pushed the wattage of her smile up a notch. "Then, I'm just in time."

Luke looked at her in puzzlement. "Time for what?"

"To take you home," she replied, as if stating the obvious, then glanced around. "Where are your clothes? I'm sure you don't want to wear that hospital gown home."

"Well, no, but—"

Spotting a narrow closet, she opened the door and found his clothes hanging inside. She carried them to the bed and handed them to him. "Do you need any help?"

A flush crawled up his neck, turning his face a bright red. "Thanks, but no. I can dress myself."

It was hard to make herself do it, but with no other options left to her, she turned to address Ry. "I'm sure you have detailed instructions to send home with him."

Ry met her gaze a moment, as if taking her measure, then lifted a shoulder and turned for the door. "They're at the nurses' station. You can pick them up there."

She frowned after him, irritated by the amusement she'd heard in his voice.

"Lauren," Luke said from behind her. "This isn't necessary. I can go home with Ry. He'll take care of me."

She whirled to confront him, her face taut with anger. "No. You're going home with me and *I'm* taking care of you."

Lauren stood before the bathroom sink, her forehead furrowed in concentration as she read over the instructions one last time.

She'd brought Luke to the cabin, rather than the lodge, insisting that he would rest better, as the cabin was quieter than the lodge. After arguing with him for a good ten minutes over him taking her bed rather than the sofa, she finally took advantage of his weakened condition and strong-armed him into her bedroom and all but shoved him into her bed.

He'd slept most of the evening while she'd finished cleaning and oiling the paneling at the lodge, and now it was time for her to perform her first nursing duty: changing his bandages.

All but sickened by the thought of causing him unnecessary pain due to her lack of experience, she pressed a shaky hand to her forehead and forced herself to read the instructions again. It seemed easy enough, she told herself. It was simply a matter of removing the present bandages, cleansing the sutured area with the solution provided, then applying fresh bandages.

Forcing a confidence to her expression that she didn't feel, she gathered the small tray of supplies and marched into the bedroom. "Ready?" she asked cheerfully.

Lying on his back, Luke struggled to a sitting position. With his back braced against the iron headboard, he tucked the sheet beneath his arms. "I feel bad about you bringing me here," he said guiltily.

"Why?" she asked, then teased him with a smile. "Are you afraid that you've put yourself in the clutches of Nurse Ratchett?"

He grinned sheepishly. "No. It's just that you've already got so much on your plate. You don't need to add taking care of me to your load."

She sat down on the side of the bed and placed the tray on the bedside table. "You're not a burden," she assured him, as she aligned her supplies. "Now," she said, and faced him. "Let's get those bandages changed."

He kept his hands fisted on the sheet he held against his chest. "It's not a pretty sight," he warned.

"I'm sure it's not, but it's got to be done."

Though she could see that he was reluctant to do so, he slowly began lowering the sheet. She noticed immediately that the soft matt of hair that had covered his chest was gone. Probably shaved off prior to his surgery, she decided.

Inch by slow inch, the bandages came into view. She gulped, wondering how painful it would be for him when she removed the tape that held them in place.

Wondering belatedly if she'd made a mistake in bringing him home with her, she lifted her gaze to his. Her uncertainties must have shown on her face, because he offered her an encouraging smile.

"You're not gonna hurt me," he assured her.

She gulped again, afraid that she would. "But what if I do? I've never done anything like this before."

"You'll do just fine." He dipped his chin and began to peel back the tape himself. "See? Painless. Doesn't hurt a bit."

Ry must have placed the sutures beneath the skin, because she could see nothing but a long, pencil-thin line of swollen flesh. "That is amazing," she murmured, awed by the sight.

"I told you. Ry's the best."

She scowled at him, then pushed his hands away to remove the remainder of the tape herself. "It's good to know that he has at least one redeeming quality," she muttered.

Fascinated by Luke's wound, she soon forgot all

about her dislike of her cousin and reached for a square of gauze and the bottle of solution. She moistened the gauze, then began to lightly stroke it over the incision.

"Does that hurt?" she asked hesitantly.

"No, ma'am. Your touch is gentle as can be."

She worked her way down the length of the incision, then started at the top again, wanting to make certain she'd cleansed it properly. Noticing a sudden tension in his chest, she lifted her gaze to his and saw that his face was flushed and his jaw was set. She immediately withdrew her hand. "I hurt you."

He shook his head. "No, ma'am. Not at all."

"There's no need to lie," she said, near tears. "If I hadn't hurt you, you wouldn't have that pained look on your face."

The flush on his face turned a shade darker. "It's not that kind of pain."

When she looked at him in confusion, he blew out a long breath.

"It's hard on a man, having a pretty woman stroke his chest."

"Oh. Well." Flustered, she tossed the soiled gauze into the wastebasket and moistened a fresh one, avoiding his gaze. "We can do this," she told him, as much to assure herself as him.

"Yes, ma'am," he said quietly. "I'll try fixin' my mind on something else."

"Good idea."

She made a quick job of completing the cleansing, then taped a new bandage in place. "There," she said, sitting back in relief. "All done."

"Almost."

"Almost? What do you mean 'almost'?"

He pushed himself to an upright position, tucking the sheet around his waist, and angled an arm behind him, pointing to a spot on the middle of his back. "Ry did a skin graft on my back. You'll need to tend that one, too. Procedure's pretty much the same as what you did to the one on my chest."

She nodded. "All right." More comfortable now with some experience under her belt, she quickly dealt with the cleansing and rebandaging of the second wound.

She straightened the supplies on the tray and stood with it, preparing to put the items away. "Are you hungry or thirsty?" she asked.

"No. Lauren?"

Already on her way to the bathroom, she stopped and glanced back. "What?"

"There's one more thing you need to do."

Dread filled her at the hesitancy in his voice. "What?"

"The skin from the graft. Ry took it from my…hip."

It took her a moment to realize what he was telling her. When she did, she sputtered a laugh, understanding now why he moved so gingerly each time he sat up. "Well, that shouldn't be too difficult," she said with a shrug.

"Easy for you to say," he said miserably. "You're not the one exposing your backside."

Biting back a smile, she set the tray on the bedside table again. "I'll close my eyes," she promised.

"Funny," he grumbled, but dutifully rolled to his side. He hiked the sheet up just high enough to expose one cheek and another bandage. "Do it quick. This is embarrassing."

Trying her best not to laugh, Lauren peeled off the tape and removed the bandage. Her amusement stayed with her, until she applied the moistened square of gauze to the wound. The minute her fingers brushed his skin, he flinched and the muscles in his buttocks went rigid as steel. His reaction was totally unexpected, and the sight unbelievably sexy. She stared, unable to tear her gaze away.

The skin on his buttocks was shades lighter than that on the rest of his body and as soft as silk, a strong contrast to the rock-hard muscles that lay beneath. Mesmerized, she dragged the back of her knuckles over him.

"Is there a problem?"

She jumped, then quickly smoothed the gauze over the wound, her face flaming in embarrassment. "No. No problem."

It was a lie. There was a problem. A *big* problem. *Lust.* She could feel it slowly spreading inside her, a molten warmth that shortened her breath and burned her eyes.

"Air," she murmured desperately, as she rubbed at her throat, thinking there wasn't enough in the room to breathe.

He glanced over his shoulder at her in confusion. "Air?"

Horrified that she'd spoken the word out loud, she snatched her hand back to clutch at her waist. "Air," she repeated, while racking her brain for a plausible explanation for having said it. "Your wound needs air," she said on sudden inspiration. "We should leave the bandage off for a while. It'll help with the healing."

Grabbing the tray, she all but ran for the bathroom and shut the door behind her. Mortified by her body's reaction to something as innocent as a bare bottom, she twisted on the tap and filled her hands with water. She splashed her face, then dropped her head to her hands on a low moan.

Had she deprived herself of sex for so long that seeing a man's naked butt turned her on? How humiliating! How pathetic!

"Lauren?"

She whirled, bracing her hands against the sink, to find Luke standing in the doorway, with the sheet wrapped around his waist.

"Are you okay?" he asked in concern.

She dipped her chin and nodded, unable to speak.

With his forehead wrinkled in concern, he crossed to her and placed a finger beneath her chin, forcing her gaze up to meet his. "You don't have to do this. I can call Ry. He'll come and get me."

She shook her head, more worried about Luke discovering what was truly wrong with her than Ry coming to her house. "No. I can do it. I just—" She gulped, wishing he wouldn't look at her so intently. Much more and she was afraid she was going to drown in the softness of his brown eyes.

"Lauren…" He eased closer, and shifted his hand to cradle her jaw.

She stared up at him, her eyes wide and unblinking. He's going to kiss me, she thought frantically. And if he didn't, she was going to have to kiss him. It would be humiliating, but how could she *not?* He was so close, his mouth so tempting, his eyes filled with such warmth, such compassion.

As she continued to meet his gaze, his eyes darkened, grew smoky. He smoothed a thumb over her lips, and her eyelids shuttered down, too heavy for her to hold up any longer.

She heard him whisper her name, then absorbed the sound as his lips captured hers.

Her bones melted. Her mind shattered. She braced a hand against his chest to remain upright and wrapped the other around his neck and clung. Every nerve in her body hummed with awareness of the body pressed to hers, her lungs filled with the breath they shared.

Perfect was all she could think. The way he kissed. The way her body molded so naturally with his. The way he held her, one hand at her cheek, the other pressed at the curve of her back, holding her to him. Gentleness and power, an unexpected blend of manliness that pleased her in a way she'd never dreamed possible.

Even as the thoughts formed he deepened the kiss, and his taste flowed through her like wine. She wanted more. Of him. Of these feelings he was awakening in her.

Who would've ever thought? she thought dreamily, as she wove her fingers through the hair at the base of his neck. She'd worked beside him, argued with him, even slept in the same cabin with him. And never once during any of that time had she ever imagined that he was capable of...*this*.

To her surprise—and utter disappointment—he chose that moment to end the kiss. She opened her eyes to find him looking at her.

He immediately dropped his gaze. "I'm sorry. I shouldn't have done that."

She looked at him curiously, wondering why he'd say such a thing, when she'd obviously enjoyed the kiss. "Well, I'm not."

He lifted his head to look at her in puzzlement. "You're not?"

Smiling, she laced her fingers behind his neck. "Not even remotely."

He dropped his forehead to hers on a groan. "You shouldn't have said that."

"And why is that?"

He pulled back to meet her gaze. "Because it makes me want to kiss you again."

"And that's a problem?"

"Damn right it is," he said in frustration. "Another five minutes and I'm going to fall flat on my face."

Her eyes widened in alarm. "Are you feeling faint?"

"No. Pain pill. I took one just before you came in and I'm already beginning to feel woozy. Another five minutes, and I'm gonna be out like a light."

He sounded so disappointed, she had to laugh.

"It's not funny," he said miserably. "Here I have your full permission to kiss you again and I'm not gonna be able to stay awake long enough to enjoy it."

Noticing that his speech was beginning to sound a bit slurred, she looped her arm through his and guided him back to the bedroom. "Who says you can't? We just need to make a few adjustments first." She urged him down on the bed, then fluffed pillows behind his head. "Comfy?" she asked.

At his nod, she crawled onto the bed and stretched out beside him, resting her head in the curve of his arm.

"Now about that kiss…" she began, and glanced over at him and smiled.

His grin lopsided, he cupped a hand at her cheek. "You're really somethin', you know that?"

"No, but you can tell me about it later."

He lowered his face to hers, but stopped just short of kissing her. "If I keel over in the middle of this, you won't be insulted, will you?"

"Only if you snore."

He choked a laugh, then winced and pressed a hand against the bandage on his chest. "No more jokes. Please. You're gonna make me bust open a stitch."

She shifted to her knees and leaned close to his face. "You're wasting precious minutes with all this talking," she scolded, as she forced him back to the pillows. "Now, shut up and pucker up."

He let his arms fall open on the bed, as if offering himself to her as a sacrifice. "Be gentle," he begged. "Remember. I'm a weak man."

Recuperation this time around was much easier for Luke to endure than the periods following his previous surgeries. Since the procedures were basically the same, he had to believe that it was Lauren who made the difference now. Being holed up in a cabin with her for three days was certainly no burden. His only complaint—if he had one—was the time she spent at the lodge preparing for the hunters. Luke didn't know the men who'd booked the reservations, but he'd already developed a dislike for them, for no other reason than they robbed him of time he could've spent with Lauren.

He wasn't a fool. He knew that when he went for his checkup tomorrow and Ry gave him the go-ahead to return to his normal activities, he'd no longer have a reason to sleep in her bed. It gave him a bad case of the blues to even think about it.

When Lauren had insisted on bringing him home with her to convalesce, he'd never dreamed he'd end up sleeping with her. Not that anything had happened between them. Some pretty serious kissing and cuddling, but that was about it. He'd have liked to have done more, but Lauren kept a tight rein on how far she'd let things go, fearing he'd hurt himself somehow if they did anything more strenuous than kiss.

As frustrating as it had been for him sexually, he wouldn't trade the past three days for anything. Not gold or power or fame. Going to sleep with her curled against his side and waking up with her still there in the morning…well, a man could get used to that kind of closeness, that kind of contentment. He'd never experienced anything like it before in his life. Not even as a boy, when he'd still lived at home with his parents, had he ever felt this sense of completeness, this sense of oneness.

Feeling the blue mood slipping over him, he pushed from the sofa and crossed to the window to look outside, determined to shake the melancholy, before it sucked him under.

The lodge stood in the distance, its tin roof gleaming like polished silver in the bright sunlight. It never ceased to amaze him, the amount of work they'd accomplished in such a short period of time. He remembered the day he'd come to apply for the handyman job, not so many weeks before. The lodge had looked rough then, still holding on to the abandoned look that had clung to it for more years than he could recall. But through hard work and sheer determination, Lauren had given the place a face-lift, returning to the building some of its old glory. There was work yet to be done, he knew. But the bulk of it was completed.

She had to be proud of her accomplishment, he thought. He knew he was proud of the small part he'd played in the restoration. There was a sense of satisfaction in giving life to something that was considered worthless and forgotten. The feeling was much the same as what he experienced when he patched up a stray or nursed a head of livestock back to good health. Saving something was saving something, whether it was a living being or a thing.

As he stared at the building, a figure passed by one of the windows and he recognized it as Lauren. He bit back a smile. No telling what she was up to today. Probably putting perfumed sachets beneath the pillows the hunters would be sleeping on. The woman was hell on details.

Suddenly hungry to see her, he grabbed his hat and stepped outside. It was his first venture outdoors since leaving the hospital, and he paused a moment, almost blinded by the bright sunlight. After snugging his hat over his head to shade his face, he shoved his hands in his pockets and headed for the lodge.

When he stepped into the kitchen, Rhena turned from the stove to peer at him.

Setting aside the spoon she held, she caught her

apron up in her hands and beamed at him as she dried them. "Well, look who's here," she teased. "I thought sure Lauren's nursing had killed you, and she'd buried the body so the vultures wouldn't give her away."

He dragged off his hat, hiding his smile. "No, ma'am. She's taken good care of me."

"Judging by that gleam in your eye, I'd say she's done better than that." She chuckled, seemingly amused by his embarrassment, and gave him a quick hug. "You look good, Luke. Downright handsome."

He shook his head. "Thank you for saying so, ma'am, but I was never handsome. Even before the fire."

"Shows how much you know," she scolded. "Handsomeness isn't something that can be physically changed. It's something inside a person. An inner glow that comes from being happy and content."

He lifted a shoulder. "I'm that, all right. Couldn't be anything else, what with all the spoiling and pampering Lauren's given me."

Lifting a brow, she turned back to the stove. "You must've returned the favor, 'cause she's wearing that same glow."

Luke frowned in puzzlement, not sure how he was supposed to take that comment. Before he could decide, Lauren sailed into the kitchen, carrying a large stack of towels. When she saw Luke, her eyes went wide.

"What are you doing up and walking around! You should be resting."

He shook his head. "I've had all the rest I can handle. Much more, and I'll petrify."

She set the towels down and hustled him to the table

and down onto a chair. "If you wanted to come to the lodge, you should have called me. I would've driven down to the cabin and picked you up."

"It's not that far a walk. The exercise did me good."

Unconvinced, she fussed with his hair, smoothing the crease his hat had put in it. "That's to be seen. You're still weak. What if you'd fainted? You could've fallen and hurt yourself."

Annoyed that she'd think he was weak, he ducked away from her hand. "I'm not weak. I'm strong as an ox, and going stir-crazy in that cabin. I need a job. Something to do."

"What you *need*," she informed him, "is to get back in bed."

Rhena elbowed her way between them and plunked a bag of apples on the table in front of Luke. "Not much fun to be in bed, if you're not there with him," she said to Lauren, then winked at Luke and handed him a knife. "Peel those apples. It'll keep your mind off what ails you."

When they returned to the cabin later that night, Lauren switched on the lamp by the sofa, then turned and watched Luke hang up his hat. "Are you tired?" she asked in concern.

He shrugged. "Not so much."

Pursing her lips, she took him by the hand. "I knew you'd overdone it," she lectured as she marched him to the bedroom. "How many times did I tell you to sit down and rest?"

Luke had had about all the mother-henning a man

could take. He snatched his hand from hers. "I'm not that kind of tired," he said in frustration. "I'm the normal kind of tired a person gets at this time of night."

Ignoring him, she pulled back the covers. "Just the same, you're going to bed. I don't want to take a chance on you having a relapse."

"Relapse?" he repeated, his anger spiraling. "How the hell can I have a relapse when I was never sick in the first place!"

She turned to look at him, as if shocked by his anger. "Are you yelling at me?"

"You're damn straight I am," he shouted. "I'm not sick. I'm not weak. And I sure as hell don't need any more rest. I've spent more time in bed over the last three days than I normally would in a month. And I don't want you fussing over me anymore," he continued, unable to stop himself. "I'm not a child, who needs lookin' after. I'm a grown man and can look out for myself."

She jutted her chin. "Well, excuse me for caring."

Seeing the gleam of tears in her eyes, Luke realized that he'd hurt her feelings. "I didn't mean that to come out the way it did," he said miserably, then heaved a breath and dropped his head. "I appreciate all you've done for me. I really do. It's just that—"

He stopped, suddenly realizing why he was angry. It wasn't because Lauren was mother-henning him to death. It was because, after tomorrow, he wouldn't be around for her to mother-hen anymore. The repairs were done. The vandal seemed to be gone. There was no reason for him to stay any longer. He was going home. Back to the bunkhouse and the empty life he'd known before Lauren.

"That *what?*" she asked defiantly.

He dragged a hand down his face, knowing he couldn't tell her the real reason for his anger. He'd fallen in love with her. It was as simple as that. But he couldn't tell her how he felt about her. If he did, it would ruin whatever chance he had left of being her friend.

"Nothing," he said wearily, and turned for the door. "I'll sleep on the sofa tonight."

Seven

Luke might claim not to be sick, but Lauren had never felt more ill in her life. Her eyes burned, her head ached and her stomach felt as if it was tied in knots.

She glanced over at his empty side of the bed, then to the twisted mess she'd made of her sheets before looking away, her eyes filling with tears. What had she done that would make him so mad? she asked herself for at least the hundredth time since Luke had left, saying he was going to sleep on the sofa. She'd spent hours going over the events of the day, trying to think of anything that she'd done or said that might've set him off. For the life of her, she couldn't think of a thing that would spawn the level of anger he'd displayed!

Maybe she'd pampered him a bit too much, she thought guiltily. But she honestly didn't think she'd treated him any differently than she had the previous two days, and he certainly hadn't complained any then. In fact, he'd seemed to like the attention she gave him. Even thrived on it!

So what had happened? she asked herself. What had she done or said that had made him so angry?

Discovering that she'd circled right back to her original question, she filled her hands with her hair. I can't stand this anymore, she thought in desperation, not knowing what she'd done, what she'd said. She dropped her hands and glanced at the door Luke had closed between them. Her fingers curled into fists. He's the one with all the answers, she thought angrily. And by golly, he was going to share them with her.

With her jaw set in determination, she marched into the den. The room was dark, but she could see the shadowed hump of his body on the sofa. Crossing to stand over him, she said, "Luke?"

He rolled to his stomach and pulled the pillow over his head.

"Luke!" she shouted.

He jumped right up off the sofa, naked as the day he was born. "What happened?" he asked, looking wildly around.

She kept her eyes riveted on his, determined not to let her gaze slide to his waist…or lower. "I can't sleep."

He sagged down to the sofa, obviously relieved that a burglar hadn't broken into the cabin while he was unawares. Catching her hand, he tugged her down beside him. "Are you sick?"

"No."

He cut her a sideways glance. "Then what's the problem?"

"You."

He stared at her a moment, then sank deeper into the sofa with a sigh. "Because I yelled at you."

"Partly," she conceded.

"I'm sorry. I told you I didn't mean what I said to come out like it did."

She glared at him over her shoulder. "And just exactly what is *that* supposed to mean? You didn't mean what you said? Or you regret the tone you used?"

He heaved another sigh and hauled her back beside him so that he could see her. "Neither. I was just mad and took it out on you."

"Mad about what?" she asked in growing frustration. "I've racked my brain for hours trying to figure out what I did or said to make you so angry and I can't come up with a single thing."

He shook his head wearily. "It's not you."

At the end of her patience, she reached over and switched on the lamp, then whirled to face him. "Then what is it? And don't tell me it's nothing, because I know darn good and well that something is bothering you. You yelled at me. Yelled!" she all but screamed. "And you've never so much as raised your voice to me before."

He lowered his gaze and clasped her hand in his on his thigh. "I have a doctor's appointment in the morning."

"So? You've known that for days. You made the appointment before you left the hospital."

"Yeah. But I didn't know then what I know now."

She huffed impatiently. "Luke, you're not making any sense."

"Tomorrow Ry is going to examine me, tell me everything's fine, and clear me to return to my normal activities."

She looked at him incredulously. "And that's a bad thing? I'd think you'd be thrilled to hear that news. You said yourself that you're going stir crazy sitting around here all day."

He lifted his head and met her gaze. "It means I'll be going home. There won't be any reason for me to stay with you any longer. The remodeling is finished and it appears the vandal who was bothering you has either given up or moved on."

She stared, stunned by the misery in his expression and by the idea that he was leaving. She'd never given any thought to how long he would stay. She'd been so consumed with her work at the lodge and caring for him that she'd focused only on the current moment and whatever needed to be done.

"I'm sorry I yelled at you," he continued. "I didn't mean to. You sure as heck didn't deserve it. Not after all you've done for me. It was just that—" He lifted a hand, then let it drop. "I was mad. Watching you turn down that bed, all I could think about was that I wouldn't be sharing it with you anymore. That I wouldn't be sleeping with you, curled up by side or waking up with you in the morning. I'll miss that. No," he corrected, shaking his head. "It's more than that." He heaved a frustrated breath. "But there's just not a strong enough word to describe the loss I'll feel."

"Oh, Luke," she murmured tearfully, cupping a hand at his cheek. "That's the sweetest thing anyone has ever said to me."

He closed his hand over hers and held it against his cheek. "It's the truth. Kissing you and holding you without being able to take it any further was pure torture. But I wouldn't trade those nights for anything."

Tears burned her throat at the openness of his admission, the honesty with which he'd shared his feelings. Oddly, she'd felt much the same way. It would've been so easy to let the kissing lead to more. She'd told herself it was her fear of him hurting himself that had kept her from succumbing to temptation. But she knew that wasn't true. She'd been burned once by a man and it was the fear of being burned again that had held her back.

But Luke was nothing like Devon, she reminded herself. In every way that Devon had failed her, Luke had supported her. He was honest, loyal, dependable, giving.

"We still have tonight," she said hopefully.

His smile sad, he released her hand and shook his head. "It would only make leaving harder. You're way out of my league, Lauren. We both know that."

She wasn't stupid. She knew he was referring to the fact that she was a Tanner and all that went with the name. But she suspected he was referring to more than simply their lifestyles. She'd seen enough evidence of his insecurities to know that he considered himself physically unattractive.

And it was up to her to prove to him that he was wrong.

Keeping her gaze on his, she slowly twisted around onto her knees to face him and placed a finger beneath his chin. "That first night you kissed me," she said softly, "I remember thinking how perfect it all was." She let her gaze slide to his mouth and trailed a finger over his lips. "The way your lips felt on mine. The way our bodies seemed to fit so naturally." She looked up at him and smiled, remembering. "Gentleness and power. That's what I sensed in you. In the way you held me. Not too tight, but with enough assurance that I felt... protected. Safe somehow. It aroused me. *You* aroused me," she clarified. "I wanted to make love with you so badly then. Even more so the next night, when we were lying in bed together and you were holding me."

She shook her head at the memory, her smile turning sheepish. "I don't think I slept at all that night. Instead I watched you sleep. Listened to you breathe. It was soothing. Comforting." She inched closer, stroked a finger over his brow. "But it was also the most frustrating night I've ever endured. The whole time I was watching you, I was wishing you'd wake up and make love with me."

His gaze locked on hers, he released a long, shaky breath. "This probably isn't wise. Talking like this, I mean. It's not going to do anything but drive us both crazy."

Her smile knowing, she slipped her hand behind his neck and drew his face to hers. "Then let's don't talk anymore."

The moment her mouth touched his, Luke knew he was lost. There was no way in hell he was going to be able to stop at just kissing her. Not this time.

With a low groan, he dragged her onto his lap, then

swept her hair back, fisting it in his hands, as he took the kiss deeper. Every word she'd spoken, every memory she'd shared had been like foreplay, teasing fingers that stroked his flesh, making his blood run hot, his body grow rigid with need.

She'd claimed his gentleness and power had aroused her. He just prayed she'd forgive him the lack of gentleness this one time. Gentleness took time and willpower, two factors he was desperately short on at the moment. What he needed—wanted—was *her.* Beneath him or on top didn't matter. He wanted inside her.

Dragging her nightgown up her legs, he lifted her and settled her over him, fitting her knees snugly at his thighs. Pleasure knifed through him as his sex brushed her moist opening, and he had to clamp his jaw down hard to keep from spilling his seed right then and there.

He dropped his head back with a moan, reminded of the chance they were taking. "Lauren, wait," he said, and gripped her hips to keep her from moving. "I don't have any protection."

She found his mouth again. "It's okay," she murmured against his lips. "I'm on the pill."

Relieved, he loosened his grip on her hips and she sank down, took him in. His body jerked instinctively, as her velvety heat closed around him like a glove. Before he could draw a full breath, she was teasing his lips apart with her tongue. Then she was riding him, matching the rhythm of her hips with that of her tongue.

He couldn't recall ever experiencing need like this. It was as if every cell of his being had gathered at the spot where their bodies were joined. His skin was on fire, his lungs ready to explode, his legs and arms quivering like plucked strings.

"Come with me," she urged against his mouth.

The warmth of her breath, the urgency in her voice was all it took to send him flying over the edge. Determined to take her with him, he drove deep with a growl. Her spine arched like a bow and her head fell back, her hair a curtain of black satin that brushed his thighs.

He saw the slow, satisfied smile that curved her lips, heard the hum of pleasure that vibrated in her throat. Then she was drifting down, melting against him, looping her arms around his neck. Her lips touched his and she exhaled a long, sated breath, whispering his name. The sweetness, the contentment in the sound wrapped itself around his chest, squeezed his heart.

Hugging her close, he buried his face in the curve of her neck…and tried his best not to think about tomorrow.

Beyond the bedroom window, the horizon was striped with dark bands of purple, pinks and blues, a sure sign that the sun would be up soon. Luke watched the colorful display over Lauren's shoulder, their bodies spooned, his arms wrapped around her. He could feel the rhythmic beat of her heart beneath his hand, hear the evenness of her breathing and was sure she was still asleep. He couldn't have slept if someone had paid him. His mind and heart were so twisted up, rest was impossible. The night had changed everything, just as he'd claimed it would. Leaving Lauren now, after having made love with her, would be even harder for him to do.

But what other choice did he have? he asked himself. He would never fit into her world any more than she'd fit into his. She was silk to his cotton. A diamond to his chunk of coal. A woman like her would be better off with a lawyer or a banker or some other high roller, who could give her the things she needed, provide her the lifestyle she was accustomed to living. Someone with a handsome face to match the beauty of hers.

He bet her ex was just such a man.

He scowled at the thought of her ex, not liking the idea of someone having lain with her, as he was now. Jealousy was an ugly emotion and one he'd never experienced before.

But it held him in its grips now.

Had she loved her ex-husband? he wondered. Did she love him still?

"Luke?"

Startled, he shoved aside his thoughts and the resentment they'd drawn. "What?"

"You're squeezing me too tight."

He immediately loosened his arm around her, unaware that his thoughts had caused the possessive action. "Sorry."

Turning within his arms, she looked up at him, then pressed a finger against the crease between his brows. "What's wrong?" she asked in concern.

He forced a smile and drew her hand to his lips. "Nothing. I was just thinking."

"You're not worried about your appointment today, are you?"

"No. I'd know if something had gone wrong with the surgery."

"Then what's bothering you?"

He knew the uncertainty would gnaw at him until he resolved the questions in his mind. "You were married before," he said hesitantly.

"Yeah. So what? I'm not now."

"Did you love him?"

"I did in the beginning, but Devon destroyed whatever feelings I had for him."

"How?"

"Lying, cheating, stealing. My father set up a trust for me and I probably could've lived off it for the rest of my life, without ever having to lift a finger. Devon insisted upon managing my investments and, like a fool, I let him. Now it's gone. Every penny. He squandered it on himself and the women I discovered he liked to entertain." She lifted a shoulder. "I trusted him and he destroyed that trust, along with whatever love I felt for him."

Luke had hoped that knowing about her past would relieve the uncertainties in his mind, but if anything, Lauren's revelation made things worse.

"No," he said slowly. "I doubt you could love a man who'd deceived you."

"There's no sense arguing with me about this, Luke," Lauren said, as she strode for her car later that morning. "I'm driving you to your appointment."

"But you've got things to do," he argued.

"I'll do them when we get back."

"I can give Monty a call and he'll come and get me. My truck's at the hospital. He wouldn't even have to stay to drive me home."

She stopped beside her car and glared at him over its roof. "There's no reason for Monty to drive all the way over here, when I'm right here and can take you." She yanked open her door. "Now get in or we're going to be late."

Scowling, he climbed into the passenger seat and jerked the seat belt across his chest. "Stubborn woman," he muttered under his breath, as he fastened the belt into place.

"Mule-headed man," she returned, and angled her head to look behind her as she backed the car down the drive.

Luke folded his arms across his chest and glared straight ahead. As she passed the lodge, he caught a flash of movement to his left and glanced that way. He froze, when he saw a partially gutted deer swinging from a rope tied to a tree limb in front of the lodge.

He grabbed Lauren's arm. "Stop."

Irritated, she tried to shake free. "I'm taking you to the dang doctor, so you might as well sit back and enjoy the ride."

He dug his fingers into her arm. "Dammit, I said stop!"

She stomped on the brakes so hard, he had to brace a hand against the dash to halt his forward thrust.

"Fine," she snapped and shoved the gearshift into Park. "Drive yourself to the doctor. See if I care."

She shouldered open her door and Luke grabbed for her, trying to keep her from climbing out, but she broke free. He bolted from the car, hoping to stop her before she saw the gutted deer. But just as he rounded the hood, he heard her shocked gasp, saw the blood drain from her face. A heartbeat later, he had her in his arms, her face pressed to his chest.

She curled her fingers into his shirt and clung. "Oh, my God, Luke," she cried, her body trembling uncontrollably. "Why? Who?"

He narrowed his gaze on the deer and shook his head. "I don't know." He stared a moment longer, trying to imagine who would do such a cruel thing, then tucked Lauren against his side and headed for the rear of the lodge, using his body to block her from the sight of the carnage.

Returning to his own home became a nonoption for Luke following the discovery of the deer. There was no way he was going to leave Lauren and Rhena alone with some "nut case," as Rhena had labeled the vandal, on the loose.

After returning from his doctor's appointment, he'd cut down the deer and disposed of the carcass. But he hadn't been able to erase the haunted look that seeing the carnage had left in Lauren's eyes. Nor had he been able to persuade her to call the sheriff, as she held firm to her belief that it was the Tanner brothers who were behind the recent mischief.

Along with Luke's frustration came an equal measure of guilt. Twice, while Ry was giving him his postoperative exam, Luke had almost told him about the happenings at the lodge. Both times he'd let the opportunity pass, his loyalty to Lauren overpowering that which he felt toward Ry. As a result, guilt weighed heavily on him, for he owed Ry a lot.

He opened his hands and stared at them, seeing them as they'd looked following the fire. The charred, black skin. The sickening odor of burned flesh. Through a cloud of drugs, he remembered hearing the nurses whispering about possible amputation. The entire hand? Maybe only his fingers? To Luke, it wouldn't have made any difference what they cut off, as the end result would've been the same. Without the use of his hands, they might as well shoot him, because he had no other skills to fall back on.

"What are you doing?"

He flinched at the sound of Lauren's voice, then dropped his hands to his thighs and rubbed them against his jeans. "Nothing."

She sank down on the sofa beside him. "If your hands are feeling dry or itchy, I could rub some cream on them for you."

He pushed to his feet and crossed to the fireplace to poke at the fire, not wanting her to see the lie in his eyes. "They're okay."

Knowing he'd been abrupt with her, he turned and stretched, faking a yawn. "You about ready to turn in? It's been a long day. I'm beat."

She picked up a magazine and shook her head. "Go ahead if you want. I'm not really sleepy."

It was a lie and he knew it, but he understood her reluctance to go to bed. Almost a month had passed since the breaking of the window and he was sure that she must have begun to feel safe again. Discovering the deer had left her feeling exposed.

"How about a hot bath?" he suggested. "That ought to make you sleepy."

She considered his suggestion a moment, then shook her head. "No. The bathroom is too close to the bedroom. It would keep you awake."

He crossed to her and scooped her up into his arms.

"Luke!" she cried, and had to drop the magazine in order to hold on to him. "What are you doing?"

"Can't keep me awake if I'm in the tub with you," he told her as he strode to the bedroom.

"But you're tired. You said so yourself."

He nudged the bathroom door open with his foot. "Never too tired to take a bath with a pretty lady."

He set her on her feet, then stooped to set the plug. "Do you have any of that bubbly stuff? And maybe some candles?"

"Luke, this really isn't necessary."

He twisted on the taps, then straightened, unbuttoning his shirt. "Says who?" When she merely frowned at him, he lifted a brow in warning. "Better start stripping. Last one in has to scrub the other's back."

Lauren pressed her toe to a bubble and popped it against the side of the tub. "You aren't fooling me for a minute. I know what you're doing."

Luke wrapped his arms around her from behind and slid farther down into the water. "And what's that?"

"You're trying to get my mind off what happened today."

Smiling, he nuzzled her ear. "Is it working?"

It was, but she wasn't about to admit that to him.

"Maybe," she said evasively and popped another bubble. "It's too soon to tell yet."

He lifted his hands to her shoulders. "I'll help things along. Close your eyes."

She did as he instructed, then moaned softly when he began to massage her tense muscles.

"Feel good?" he asked.

"Better than good."

He worked his way down her arms, loosening muscles she hadn't even known were taut. His touch was strong, capable, soothing. Feeling mellow, she laid her head back to rest on his chest. "If I go to sleep," she murmured, "promise you won't take advantage of me."

"That's sure askin' a lot of a man."

She smiled softly. "Not this man. You're much too honorable to take advantage of a defenseless woman."

He slid his hands up her stomach and cupped her breasts. "Maybe you better stay awake then. I wouldn't want to destroy your image of me."

She shivered, as he stroked his thumbs over her nipples. "I don't think you could."

"Every man is capable of a fall," he warned.

She tipped her head back and pressed a kiss to the underside of his chin. "Not you. You're special."

His hands stilled a moment, then he began to massage her breasts. "I hope I never do anything to make you think different."

"You're very good at that."

"What?"

She laid a hand over his. "This."

As he continued to stroke her breasts, an ache sprang to life between her legs and she moaned softly, squeezing her knees together in an effort to ease it. As if sensing her need, he slid a hand down her abdomen and cupped her mound. She tensed at the delicious pressure, then sighed, parting her legs for him. He pushed a knuckle down her fold, then straightened his finger and dragged it back up the crease, until she was moist and throbbing.

"Luke," she said breathlessly and reached a hand up to touch his face. "Please."

He pressed his lips to her ear. "Please, what?"

She clamped her knees together, sure that she'd die from the pressure building inside her.

"Love me," she begged. "Please love me."

"Hard to do much else." He lifted her up higher on his chest and guided his sex to her opening. "Wrap your arms around my neck."

Willing to do anything he asked, she reached up and behind her and locked her fingers behind his neck.

"Don't let go," he ordered softly. "No matter how much you want to, hold on to me and keep your eyes closed."

Positioned as she was, she felt exposed, vulnerable, but nodded, knowing she could trust him.

He cupped her breasts and began to stroke. With her eyes closed, she couldn't anticipate his movements, only feel. Each new place he touched her was a shock to her system initially, then was followed by the most delicious swell of sensation that spread through her body in wave after wave of excruciating pleasure. Her nipples ached, her womb throbbed.

She could feel the prod of his sex lengthening and thickening against her bottom and strained, fighting the desire to free her hands so that she could touch him, too.

"Luke," she begged, gasping.

His tip nudged her center, the pressure a promise of strength and power that she all but wept for, would beg for if he asked her to. He entered her an inch. Another. Impatient, she bore down and swallowed a cry of pleasure as she took in his entire length.

Color exploded behind her eyelids, brilliant shards of red, gold and silver, as she came apart around him. "Luke!" she cried, arching high.

He wrapped his arms tightly around her and buried his face at the base of her neck. "It's okay, baby," he soothed. "I've got you. I'm right here with you."

Even as he offered the reassurance, his body went rigid and his fingers dug into her hips, holding her against him. At the first warm spurt of his climax, she unlaced her fingers and brought her hands around to his cheeks. She sensed the leashed power within his body in the clenched muscles of his jaw, the amount of strength his release cost him in the spasms that shook his body.

When he stilled, she slowly blinked open her eyes, both humbled and awed by the experience. Wanting—*needing*—to see him, to touch him, she turned, creating a tidal wave of bubbles and water that spilled over the sides of the tub.

She brushed a finger over his cheek, and he opened his eyes to meet her gaze.

"Oh, Luke," she whispered, "I've never experienced anything like that. The sensations…with my eyes closed, it was like everything was magnified a hundred times."

His smile soft, he reached to tuck a lock of hair behind her ear. "That's the point. When you can't see, you become more aware of your other senses."

She stilled and searched his gaze. "The fire. You knew that because of the fire."

He nodded. "My whole head was bandaged for a while. Couldn't see so much as a shadow, the gauze was so thick. It was scary at first. Not knowing who was in the room with you, or if there was anyone at all, or what they were doing to you. I learned to use my other senses. Let *them* be my eyes."

She traced a finger below his lashes, her heart breaking at all he'd suffered. "I can't imagine how awful that must have been."

"It was bad. I'd be lying if I said it wasn't. But the people who cared for me were kind. Tried their hardest to make the treatments as bearable for me as they could."

Saddened by all the pain he'd endured, she wrapped her arms around his neck and laid her cheek against his chest. "I wish I had known you then. I would have taken care of you."

He pressed a kiss to the top of her head. "You couldn't have done anything."

She lifted her head and met his gaze, unashamed of the tears that glistened in her eyes. "But I could've been there for you. Held your hand when you were scared."

He cupped a hand at her cheek. "Just knowin' you would have done that for me pleases me more than you'll ever know." Grinning, he winked at her. "Now let's get out of this tub before we both turn into prunes."

He braced his hands on the sides of the tub and started to push himself up, but she pressed a hand against his chest, stopping him.

"Luke…" She gulped, knowing she had to share with him what was in her heart. "I…I think I'm falling in love with you."

He grew still as death, then slowly sank back into the water, his eyes fixed on hers. "Sometimes people mistake pity for love."

That he would think pity was what she felt for him nearly broke her heart. "It isn't pity," she assured him. "I…I'm not sure I can explain it, the when or why of it. But I know I want to be with you. When I am, I feel complete. Happy. Content."

"I feel the same way." When she would've said something, he pressed a finger to her lips, silencing her. "But you're not thinking this through, Lauren. I told you before you're way out of my league, and I meant it. I'm a cowboy. I wouldn't know how to be anything else. I dropped out of school in my junior year. I don't even have a high school degree."

"Do you think that matters to me? A piece of paper isn't what makes a man." She laid her hand over his heart. "It's what's in here that counts. You're gentle, kind, honest, sincere. That's what makes me love you, Luke. Not what degrees you might have earned or how much money you make. It's *you* I love."

He gathered her into his arms and held her tight. "I love you, too. But just know that if you should ever change your mind, I'll understand."

Pulling back, she gathered his face between her hands and looked deeply into his eyes. "I'm not going to change my mind, Luke. I'll always love you."

Eight

Lauren all but danced into the kitchen at the lodge, her cheeks flushed and her eyes glowing.

"Good morning, Rhena," she called cheerfully.

Rhena scowled. "I don't know what's so good about it. That dang dog of yours kept me up half the night."

When Lauren brought Luke home from the hospital, she'd insisted upon Buddy staying at the lodge, fearing in his exuberance, he'd somehow hurt Luke. Concerned, she looked at Rhena. "Is Buddy sick?"

"No. He wanted to sleep in bed with me and wouldn't take no for an answer."

Knowing how much Rhena disapproved of a dog sleeping in a bed, Lauren sputtered a laugh, imagining the battle that had ensued during the night. "Who won?"

"Who do you think? He's bigger than me." She continued to scowl, and scrubbed harder at the pan. "And he's a bed hog. Kept pushing until he had me all but hanging by my fingernails off the side of the mattress."

Laughing, Lauren hugged Rhena to her side. "That's a man for you. Luke's the same way."

Rhena lifted a brow. "So you're sleeping with him?"

Lauren sighed dramatically. "Not only that, I'm in love with him."

Rhena nodded in approval. "You could do worse. Luke's a good man."

"The best," Lauren corrected, then smiled. "I don't think he's accepted the idea yet, but he'll come around."

Rhena looked at her in puzzlement. "He doesn't share your feelings?"

"Oh, he loves me," Lauren assured her. "He's just having a hard time believing that I really love him."

Rhena snorted. "That man's blind when it comes to his own worth. I swear that fire must have burned his ego plumb out of him."

"His worst scars aren't the visible ones," Lauren agreed. "Emotionally, he's got some healing to do yet."

"He's come a long way, just since he's been hanging around here. He's quit wearing his gloves all the time, and he doesn't hide his face beneath his hat like he used to."

"It still amazes me that he thought his face was anything to be ashamed of," Lauren said.

"Ry did a good job on him, no doubt about that."

At the mention of Ry, Lauren frowned and glanced at her watch, reminded of her purpose in stopping in at the lodge. "I'm going to have to hurry if I hope to catch him."

"Catch who? Luke?"

Lauren's frown deepened. "No. Ry. I've decided it's time for a showdown. Our hunters are scheduled to arrive in a few days and I don't want to take a chance on the Tanners causing any trouble while they're here."

Rhena looked at her doubtfully. "Do you really think the Tanners are the ones behind all this? The few times I've been around Buck's sons, they seemed like nice enough men."

"Who else would want to scare me off?" Lauren challenged. "Buck fought with my dad over this property from the day my grandfather willed it to my father, and now that Buck's gone, his sons have taken up the sword. They think if they intimidate me long enough, I'll tuck my tail between my legs and run back to Dallas." She set her jaw in determination. "But they're wrong. I don't scare easily."

Rhena set aside her dishcloth and reached behind her to untie her apron. "Give me a minute to get my purse, and I'll go with you."

"No," Lauren told her. "I'm doing this alone."

"Then take Luke," Rhena urged. "It wouldn't hurt to have some muscle to back you up."

Already turning away, Lauren fluttered a hand. "Can't. Monty picked him up early this morning and took him to get his truck."

The Tanner ranch was everything Lauren remembered it to be and more. The last time she'd paid a visit to her uncle and his sons, she'd been about four years old. Rhena had often referred to the trip as Lauren's father's last-ditch effort to reconcile with his brother

Buck. Lauren remembered the visit only as a nightmare. The yelling and cursing between the two men had frightened her, and she'd hidden in a closet and covered her ears with her hands. Ace, Buck's oldest son, had found her there and drawn her outside with the promise of showing her his new puppy. She'd stayed with Ace in the barn until her father had come to collect her for the drive home.

At the age of four, the house had seemed massive to her. With the advantage of twenty-plus years, her opinion remained the same. Though actually not much larger than her father's home in Dallas, the Tanner homestead seemed much bigger, as all the rooms were located on one floor, whereas those in her father's home were scattered over three stories. She remembered her father telling her that the space used as the den and living room dated back to the 1800s and was the original Tanner home. Additions had been made over the years as the wealth and size of the family increased. The result was a sprawling log-and-stone house as impressive in design as it was in size.

But as Lauren stood before the front door, waiting for someone inside to respond to her knock, she wasn't thinking about the size of the house or its design. Her thoughts were filled with hate for Buck Tanner's sons.

At last the door opened. A woman peered at Lauren curiously. "Can I help you?"

"I'm here to see Ry," she replied.

"He's not here at the moment. They had a problem at the barn. A cow's having trouble delivering a calf," she explained further. She gestured inside. "Would you like to wait inside? He shouldn't be long."

Determined to have it out with Ry once and for all, Lauren shook her head. "Thanks, but I'll go to the barn."

She returned to her car and drove the short distance to the barn. Taking a deep breath, she marched inside.

"Ry?" she called "It's Lauren. I need to talk to you."

There was a rustle of movement, then Ry stepped from a stall. "Lauren?" he said in surprise, then hurried toward her, wiping his hands on the seat of his jeans. "I can't believe you're really here." He grabbed her hand and pumped it. "You should have called and told me you were coming. I could've called my brothers. I know they'd like to see you, too."

Unmoved by the friendliness of his greeting, she jerked her hand from his and clenched it at her side. "This isn't a social call."

He looked at her in puzzlement. "Is there a problem?"

"Yes," she snapped. "Mainly you and your brothers." She took a step toward him and shoved her face up close to his. "I know what y'all are trying to do and I've come to tell you that you're wasting your time. I'm not leaving, and I'm sure as heck not turning over the lodge to you."

He drew back to peer at her in confusion. "What are you talking about?"

She ticked off her grievances on her fingers. "The broken window. The dead deer you left swinging from the tree. None of it worked. You can't scare me away. I've made the lodge my home and I'm not leaving."

"We don't want you to leave," he insisted. "In fact, we're glad you moved down here."

"Yeah, right," she muttered darkly.

"It's true. We—"

"Ry, I found that antibiotic you wanted."

Lauren whirled at the sound of the voice and was stunned to see Luke striding toward them. He jerked to a stop when he saw her, obviously as shocked to see her in the Tanners' barn as she was to see him there.

"What are you doing here?" she cried.

He started toward her, his face creased with concern. "Lauren, I can explain."

Ry stepped forward. "Maybe I better. This is my fault, after all."

Lauren snapped her head around to stare at Ry. "What's your fault?"

"This…misunderstanding. My brothers had heard what your ex-husband did to you, and we were worried about you and wanted to offer our help. When you refused, we tried to think of a way to keep an eye on you, so that we would be aware of any problems you might run into. Your ad in the paper for a handyman provided us with the perfect opportunity to do just that." He gestured toward Luke. "Luke works for us here on the ranch, and we asked him to apply for the job."

Anger swelled inside her, a blinding rage that lodged in her throat and threatened to choke her. And with it a crippling sense of betrayal that threatened to drag her to her knees.

Trembling, she curled her hands into fists. "Did you pay him to spy on me?" she demanded to know.

"He wasn't spying," Ry said.

"Did you *pay* him?" she repeated, her voice rising.

His eyes widened in surprise at her anger. "Well,

yes. I guess you could say we paid him, since he was on our payroll."

"I want a complete accounting of the money he received during the time he was in my employ."

"But…why?"

"Because I intend to pay you back every red cent." Whirling, she marched for her car.

"Lauren! Wait!"

She ignored Luke's plea and opened her car door. He caught up with her and shoved a hand against it, slamming it before she could slip inside.

"Lauren, please," he begged. "Let me explain."

She drew in a deep breath, willing herself not to cry, then turned to face him. "You lied to me. Deceived me. I trusted you, even fell in love with you, and the whole time you were working for the Tanners. Was that part of the plan?" she asked bitterly. "Seduce me so that you could win my confidence? Maybe even talk me into selling the property to them?"

"Lauren, please."

When he reached for her, she jerked away.

"Don't you dare touch me," she warned. "Not ever again."

She snatched open the car door and slid inside, slamming the door behind her. She drove away, blinded by tears, sure that the sound she heard was her heart breaking.

The Tanner brothers sat around the kitchen table at the ranch house, with Ace, the accepted leader of the family since Buck's death, seated at its head. Luke sat at the opposite end, listening, as Ry relayed to his brothers Lauren's suspicion that the Tanners were spying on her.

"What happened wasn't Luke's fault," he said in summation, "though Lauren has placed the bulk of the blame on him. We were the ones who asked him to apply for the handyman job, which was the same as asking him to deceive her.

"You all know as well as I do that Luke would never purposely deceive anyone. He's not that kind of man. It was out of loyalty to the Tanner family that he agreed to our request." He glanced at Luke. "To make matters worse for him, Luke won Lauren's heart while he was working for her, and now she thinks he seduced her as part of our plan. I don't know about the rest of you, but I think we need to do something to set things right between them."

"I agree," Ace concurred, then narrowed his eyes on Luke. "But first I think Luke needs to explain to us why he never told us about the problems Lauren's been having at the lodge."

Luke dropped his gaze, uncomfortable with telling the Tanners his reason.

"Well, Luke?" Ace prodded. "That was the reason we sent you over there. Why didn't you ever tell us what's been going on over there?"

Luke lifted his head and looked Ace square in the eye. "I wanted to. I even tried to get her to come and stay here at the ranch until we could catch whoever was messing with her."

"So why didn't she?" Ace challenged.

"You tell me," Luke challenged, then rose and tossed up his hands in frustration. "She hates the whole damn lot of you. Swears you're out to get her, so that you can have the lodge."

"That's ridiculous," Ry said. "We don't want the lodge. And if we did, we'd ask her outright to sell it to us. We wouldn't be pulling these stunts, trying to scare her off."

"That's what I told her," Luke replied, then flattened his hands on the table and looked around at each of the seated men. "But you tell me who else would want her gone? She doesn't know anyone around here, other than y'all. She hasn't lived here long enough to make any enemies."

"You think we're behind this?" Ry asked in disbelief.

Luke straightened and squared his shoulders. "A month ago, I'd've coldcocked the first person foolish enough to say a bad word against a single one of you." He shook his head. "But I know Lauren. I love her. She's not the kind of woman who would hold a grudge like this unless she had good reason. So you tell me," he challenged again. "Why does she hate the Tanners so much?"

The brothers looked from one to the other. It was Ace who finally spoke.

"We don't know," he said wearily. "We assumed it stemmed from Buck trying to force Randall to sell him the lodge. But Buck's gone now, and we've never done anything to make her think we wanted the lodge. Hell," he said, in frustration, "we've done nothing but offer her our help since she moved to Tanner's Crossing!"

Silence followed Ace's impassioned speech. Rory, the youngest of the Tanner brothers and the peacemaker of the group, was the one who finally spoke.

"I think we should talk to her," he said quietly. "All of us. Clear the air. Maybe she knows something the rest of us don't. You know how Buck was," he added. "For all we know, Buck could've done or said something that's soured her on all of us."

"Like what?" Ry asked in frustration.

"Hell if I know," Rory replied with a shrug. "But knowing Buck, if he did do something, you know it was underhanded and downright mean."

After returning to the lodge after her confrontation with Luke, Lauren immersed herself in work, taking her anger out on polishing the dining room table.

"You're going to rub a hole in that wood," Rhena warned.

Lauren sniffed, but kept polishing. "I want everything to be perfect when the hunters arrive tomorrow."

"You're entertaining hunters," Rhena reminded her. "Not the Queen of England."

"All our guests deserve the same treatment, no matter what their station."

Rhena sagged her shoulders in frustration. "Talk to Luke," she begged. "I'm sure he can explain why he did what he did."

Ignoring her, Lauren asked, "Do you have the coffee cakes ready?"

Rhena heaved a sigh. "Baked and on the counter cooling."

Lauren slapped a hand to her forehead. "Cream!" she wailed. "I forgot to buy cream for the coffee."

"We'll offer them milk. They're men. They'll never know the difference."

Lauren tossed down the rag and headed for the door. "*I'll* know."

"Surely you're not going to drive all the way into town for a carton of cream?" Rhena called after her. "That's crazy."

"Crazy or not," Lauren replied, as she opened the door, "that's exactly what I'm doing." She stepped out onto the porch and groaned. "Oh, no."

"What's wrong?" Rhena asked, as she stepped out onto the porch beside her.

"We've got company."

Rhena craned her neck to peer at the trucks coming down the drive, then frowned at Lauren. "You did jot down the right date, didn't you?"

Lauren shook her head. "Those aren't our hunters coming. It's the Tanners."

Rhena lifted a brow, then shook her head and turned back into the lodge. "I'll batten down the hatches. Looks like we're in for a storm."

"Coward," Lauren muttered, then squared her shoulders, preparing herself for battle as the men climbed from their trucks.

"You're not welcome here," she said as they approached, then narrowed her eyes on Luke and added, "Especially you."

She knew he heard her, because the tips of his ears turned red, but he kept coming, the same as the others.

As if on cue, they stopped and pulled off their hats. Lauren knew a moment's unease at the sight they presented. Tall, broad-shouldered, dark-headed, the Tanner brothers formed a formidable wall of strength she doubted few men dared breach.

The man in the center stepped forward, separating himself from the others. "Lauren, I'm Ace. I doubt you remember me—"

"Rowdy," she said slowly. "That was the name of your puppy. You took me outside to show him to me because I was afraid of all the yelling."

He lifted a brow, obviously surprised that she recalled the incident. "I can't believe you remember my dog's name. You were just a little girl."

"Kindnesses are seldom forgotten." And because he'd been kind to her, she would listen to what he had to say. She opened a hand, giving her permission for them to enter. "You have ten minutes. No more."

With a nod of agreement, Ace followed her inside, his brothers and Luke falling into step behind him.

Ace stopped in the center of the main room and looked around. "You've done a good job here. If I didn't know better, I'd think I'd stepped through a time tunnel that took me back fifty years."

She gestured to the leather couches, indicating for them to be seated, then sat in a chair, separate from them. "My father neglected the lodge for too many years. Which is understandable," she added bitterly, "considering the circumstances."

Sitting, Ace hooked his hat over his knee with a sigh. "It's those circumstances that we'd like to talk to you about." He waved a hand in Luke's direction. "Luke tells us that you don't particularly care for us."

She met Ace's gaze squarely, unashamed of her feelings. "I don't. Your family has caused my family nothing but heartache."

Ace gave her a reproving look. "I don't argue that Buck could be a pain in the ass, but I hardly think him putting pressure on your father to sell him the lodge would be considered heartache."

"Really?" Lauren challenged. "I understand that you lost your mother at a young age."

"Yes. To cancer." He looked at her in puzzlement. "But what has that got to do with this?"

"I lost my mother, too, at a young age. I was twelve when she died."

He nodded sympathetically. "I understand how hard that must have been for you." He indicated his brothers. "We all do. We loved our mother very much and grieved sorely over her loss, as I'm sure you did yours."

"My mother committed suicide."

Ace frowned, obviously confused. "Surely you don't blame us for your mother's death?"

"Oh, but I do," she informed him coolly. "If not for your father, my mother would be alive today."

Ace's frown deepened and he shook his head. "I'm sorry, Lauren, I don't understand."

She rose, her body stiff with the anger and resentment she'd harbored for years. "Your father used my mother. Seduced her. Made her believe that he loved her. Promised to marry her, if she would divorce my father. He was clever," she added bitterly. "Charming. Said he would guide her through the legalities. Make sure that she received her fair share in the divorce settlement."

Unable to remain still, she paced, the memories making her restless. "The day she approached my father about the divorce, she presented him with a carefully made list of all her demands. Listed among the assets was the lodge and the acreage that my grandfather had willed to my father."

She turned then to look at Ace. "That was your father's one mistake. If he hadn't made my mother specifically request that property, my father might never have known. My father loved my mother, and because he did, he would have done anything to make her happy. Including giving her a divorce, if that was what she wanted.

"But when he saw the lodge listed, he knew that Buck was involved and that he'd used my mother to get what my father refused to give him. When he confronted her, she admitted to having an affair with Buck. He told her that Buck had used her in order to get even with him."

She inhaled a deep breath, needing the fortification it gave her, before she could tell the rest. "She shot herself. The bullet entered her skull at the right temple and penetrated the brain. It was a miracle that she didn't die instantly. Machines kept her alive for eighteen hours. It took that long for the doctors to convince my father that there were no brain waves and that she was, for all intents and purposes, dead. When he gave them permission to pull the plug, he cried. He still does. Unlike Buck, my father loved my mother. In spite of the fact that she had cheated on him with his own brother, he loved her and will until the day he dies.

"You asked me why I don't particularly care for you. Now you know why." She crossed to the door and opened it. "If you will excuse me, I have guests coming tomorrow and I need to prepare for their arrival."

"I don't blame her for hating us," Rory said. "If I were her, I'd hate us, too."

"But we had nothing to do with any of that," Woodrow argued. "That was Buck's doing, not ours."

Ace held up a hand to forestall a fight. "I agree with both of you. But her resentment is definitely understandable."

"Sins of the father," Ry muttered, then swore. "I don't know about the rest of you, but I'm damn sick and tired of paying for the old man's sins."

"And what can you do about it?" Ace challenged.

Ry rose, dragging a hand over his hair. "I don't know, but there ought to be something. The old man's dead. Why couldn't his sins have been buried with him?"

"Not enough room in the casket to hold 'em all," Woodrow said under his breath. He glanced up and caught the disapproving look Rory sent him. "Well, it's the truth," he said defensively. "We no more put out one fire he's left burnin', than another flames up for us to deal with."

"Give Lauren time," Luke suggested quietly.

"How much time does she need?" Ry asked in frustration. "Her mother's been gone more than twenty years."

"But she never had the satisfaction of spittin' in the face of the man she holds responsible," Luke replied.

"She still hasn't," Ace reminded him. "Buck's dead."

"But she had the satisfaction of tellin' her grievances to his sons. That's bound to ease her mind some."

"That's ridiculous," Woodrow scoffed.

Ace held up a hand. "No. Luke may have a point. Had we known about this, we might've been able to end this feud a long time ago. Up until now, we didn't even know why the feud was being fought. A lot of healing can take place, once the air is cleared."

"She certainly had her turn in clearin' it," Woodrow muttered disagreeably. "Didn't give us a chance to say squat in return."

"Amen to that," Whit said dryly.

"There'll be time for us to have our say in the future," Ace said. "Right now I think we need to focus on the problems she's been having at the lodge." He turned his gaze to Luke. "Do you have any idea who might be behind all this?"

Luke shook his head. "The night the rock was thrown through the window, I checked for tracks and any clues that might've been left behind. Came up with nothin'. Same with the incident with the limb fallin' on her head. I found the place on the tree where the limb was broken and marks that indicated someone had climbed the tree. But there wasn't anything to point to who did it."

"Why didn't you call the sheriff?" Ace asked.

Luke lifted a brow. "You really want to know?"

"Would I have asked if I didn't?"

Luke shrugged. "She said there was no point in calling the sheriff, because the Tanners owned the town."

"Which is the same as saying we own the sheriff, too," Ry said dryly.

Ace stood, rubbing his jaw. "I've got a bad feeling about this."

"Are you thinking she needs protection?" Rory asked.

"Wouldn't hurt," Ace replied. "She thinks we're the ones responsible for trying to run her off. Since we all know we're not, that means whoever does want her gone is still out there."

Luke stood, tugging on his hat. "I'll see that she stays safe."

Ry looked at him doubtfully. "Do you really think she's going to want you around? Because of the position we put you in, it looks as if she feels the same way about you as she does us."

"Doesn't matter what she thinks of me," Luke told him. "I won't see her hurt."

Nine

Shivering, Luke trudged through the woods, silently cursing himself for not taking the time to grab a jacket. Though the temperature during the daytime hovered in the seventies, the October nights were getting downright cold. It had to be close to forty degrees outside, and morning was still hours away.

So far, things had remained quiet around the lodge. Keeping to the shadows of the trees that surrounded it and the cabins, he'd completed several rounds of his sentry duty and hadn't seen or heard anything out of the ordinary…although Buddy had scared a good ten years off his life. Obviously let out by Rhena to take care of his business before bedtime, Buddy had scented Luke and come crashing through the woods to greet him, barking loud enough to alert the entire county. Luke had managed to quiet him down and finally convinced the dog to return to the lodge.

He knew it was selfish, but he wished Buddy was in the cabin with Lauren. Better yet, he wished Lauren was in the lodge with Buddy and Rhena. He'd feel better knowing that the three of them were together. Safety in numbers, he thought, though how effective any one of the three would be against an intruder he wasn't sure. Rhena was a tough old bird, but he figured her age alone would hinder her effectiveness in defending herself. Buddy's size would intimidate most men, but Luke wasn't sure how the dog would respond if it came to a fight. And Lauren...

He swallowed a groan, his chest tightening painfully at the thought of her. He'd lost her for good. There was no question about that. And it was his own damn fault. He'd lied to her, deceived her just as she'd accused him of doing. And he knew what she did to men who were less than honest with her. She divorced them. Or, at least, she had her ex-husband when she discovered he'd deceived her. Ridding herself of Luke had been much easier. She'd simply cut him out of her life.

He'd deserved it, he told himself. But knowing that didn't lessen the pain any. He loved her. Always would. Nothing was going to change that.

He gave himself a shake, refusing to feel sorry for himself. She'd been good to him. Good *for* him. The one thing he could do to repay her kindness was to keep her safe. To catch the person who was trying to hurt her.

And in order to do that, he had to remain alert and keep walking. Feeling sorry for himself would do nothing but distract him from the job at hand.

Coming in line with the cabin, he stopped beneath the shadow of the trees and studied the structure for any sign of foul play or disturbance. Lauren was obviously asleep, as the lights were off and the windows dark. A thin plume of smoke curled from the chimney, an indication that the fire she'd started in the fireplace still burned. He shivered again, yearning for its warmth, and remembered other fires he'd enjoyed with Lauren, curled up on the sofa with her, her body nestled against his.

Turning away from the cabin, as well as the memories it held, he forced himself to walk again, his heart heavy, his steps leaden.

Lauren dreamed of Luke, of them making love. In the dream, he lay beside her, looking down at her, his brown eyes soft with the warmth of his love. His hands, wide and powerful, stroked her body, his fingers leaving trails of fire in their wake. She loved his hands. Though he was ashamed of the scars that snaked his flesh and the gnarled shape of his fingers, she knew the tenderness within them, the quiet strength they held.

She inhaled a deep breath, gathering the sensations he strummed from her body, and held it in her lungs, wanting to capture the pleasure and make it last as long as she possibly could.

And then the dream changed and her lungs burned. There was smoke. Cloying and so thick she couldn't see. It filled her chest, squeezed her throat. A barn burned in the distance. She could see the flames licking the sky. A figure appeared in the doorway, his clothes on fire. *Luke.* As his name formed in her mind, she heard his screams.

Bloodcurdling cries of agony that resounded around and around in her mind. She began running, her heart pounding within her chest, her eyes riveted on his face and the terror and pain that twisted his features. But as hard as she ran, he remained maddeningly out of her reach. The flames leaped higher, nipping at his hair, his face.

Her lungs burned with smoke; her stomach roiled from its cloying scent. She couldn't breathe. Couldn't see. She stumbled and fell, clawing at her throat, her mouth wide and gasping. Tears streamed down her face. Luke. She had to get to Luke. Had to save him.

She sat up, yanked from the dream into wakefulness. She closed her eyes against the smoke that filled the air, sure that the dream still had her in its clutches. But when she opened them, the smoke was still there, a thick haze that shrouded her room. She coughed, choked by the acrid scent, and pushed from her bed, knowing she had to escape. She started for the door, but then stopped, staring in horror at the smoke that curled from beneath it, thickening the air.

With her hands outstretched, she turned and groped blindly for the window. Her hands struck the glass and she sagged with relief. Knowing she had to hurry, she fumbled for the lock, unfastened it, then lifted the sash.

Panic squeezed her chest when the window refused to budge. Setting her jaw, she tugged harder, putting all her strength into the effort. Choked by a sob, she sank to the floor and covered her face with her hands, knowing there was no escape. She was trapped inside.

Think, Lauren. Think!

Dropping to her hands and knees, she crawled to the

bathroom. She dragged a towel from the rack, then used the toilet as a brace to heave herself to her feet. She swayed dizzily, her stomach roiling. Pressing the towel to her mouth, she fought back the nausea that rose, then dropped the towel and sagged over the sink, retching and retching, until there was nothing left for her to throw up. Weak, her legs no longer able to support her, she crumpled to the floor.

She was going to die, she thought, and quietly accepted her fate. There was no way out of the cabin. No one to save her.

Luke. She dropped her face to her hands and wept, wishing she could tell him she was sorry. Take back all the hateful and mean things she'd said to him. Tell him one last time that she loved him.

Can't give up. There's always a reason to live.

Remembering his words, she dropped her hands. She had a reason to live. Luke had given her a reason. He'd given her his heart, his love. She couldn't give up. She wouldn't.

The window, she thought, forcing herself to think. That was her only hope of escape. She'd have to break the glass. Climb out. Overcome with smoke again, she coughed, then grabbed the towel, drenched it in water, and pressed it to her mouth.

Time was running out, she thought weakly. She was having trouble breathing. There wasn't enough air. Her arms were leaden, her vision blurry, her mind fuzzy. Sliding down to her stomach, she wrapped the towel around her fist and began to belly-crawl her way back to the bedroom, stretching one arm out, dragging herself forward, then stretching out the other. Her fingers snagged in the loops of the hand-hooked rug at the side of her bed and she knew she was close to reaching the window. Her head lolled and she tried to force it up. A few more feet, she told herself. A few more feet.

Darkness sucked at her. She was so tired. So tired. *Luke. She needed Luke.* Wanted to feel his arms around her, bury her face against his chest. She pushed out her arm, her nails clawing at the wood floor. Her head was so heavy. Too heavy to hold up. She dropped her forehead to the floor, gasping. She'd rest just a minute….

The darkness slid over, drawing her in.

Luke stopped and scrubbed his hands over his face, trying to shock himself into alertness. A couple more hours, he told himself and forced himself to push on. A couple more hours and the sun would be up and Lauren would be safe. The person trying to hurt her had always struck at night. A coward, using the cover of darkness to hide his misdeeds.

A branch snapped to his left and he whirled, bringing his shotgun to his shoulder and curling a finger around the trigger. A doe stood on the path, poised for flight, her eyes gleaming in the darkness. With a sigh, he lowered his gun and waved an impatient arm. "Go on," he muttered. "It's not you I'm hunting."

The doe bolted through the underbrush, her white tail quickly disappearing into the darkness.

Exhausted, Luke dropped down on a stump and laid his shotgun over his knees. From his position, he could just make out the top of the cabin's tin roof. Moonlight streamed over the old tin, turning it to silver. From the roof's ridge, the chimney rose, a shadowed column of native stone. Noticing that no smoke curled from the chimney, he frowned, then slowly rose. There should be smoke still. Even if the fire had burned out, the embers would still be smoking. He started walking, his gaze on the chimney. The closer he got, his steps quickened. A light was on in the bedroom, he noted. When he'd passed by the last time, the window had been dark. But the light didn't look right. It wasn't bright enough. Appeared dull, as if he were looking at it through a fog.

Not fog, he thought, fear tightening his chest. Smoke! He started running, leaping over the tangles of brush that blocked his way as he tugged his cell phone from his pocket. He punched the number of the ranch house, then held the phone near his ear, listening to the rings as he ran. Ry answered on the second ring, his voice husky with sleep.

"Lauren's hurt," he shouted. "Get an ambulance and a fire truck."

Before Ry could ask any questions, Luke tossed the phone aside and ran faster.

By the time he reached the cabin, his heart was pounding hard enough to crack bone, and his lungs were pumping like bellows. In one leap he cleared the cabin's steps and had his hand on the doorknob. Finding the door locked, he swore, then raced across the porch and jumped to the ground. He rounded the side of the cabin and skidded to a stop before the bedroom window. Using his hand as a blinder, he pressed his face against the glass.

He saw Lauren sprawled motionless on the floor and his heart seemed to stop for a moment, then kicked against his ribs. Setting his jaw, he lifted his shotgun and rammed the butt against the window. Glass and wood exploded, sending shards of debris flying, and smoke poured through the opening. Luke dropped the gun and threw an arm up to cover his face as he reached inside with his other hand to release the lock. Finding it unfastened, he shoved up the sash and swung a leg over the sill.

"Lauren!"

He dropped to a knee beside her, his eyes and lungs burning from the smoke. Not knowing whether she was injured or not, he hesitated a moment, unsure if it was safe to move her, then scooped her up into his arms and ducked through the window. Holding her tight against his chest, he dropped to the ground and ran. When he was sure he was a safe distance away from the cabin, he stopped and lowered her to the ground.

He took her face gently between his hands, blinded by tears. "Lauren," he choked out past the fear that clotted his throat, and dropped his forehead to hers. He gulped a breath, fighting back the fear, then lifted his head.

"You're going to be all right," he promised her, and began to chafe her hands. "I'm not going to lose you now."

He heard Buddy's bark and glanced up to see both the dog and Rhena racing toward him.

"What happened?" Rhena cried, as she sank to her knees beside him.

"Smoke," he gasped, as he shifted to press his hands against Lauren's chest, forcing the smoke from her lungs.

He heard a siren in the distance. "Go to the lodge and meet the ambulance," he ordered. "Show 'em the way back here."

He continued to administer CPR, alternately pumping her chest and forcing his own breath past her lips, until the paramedics arrived. When they did, he was shoved out of the way and stood helplessly by, watching as the paramedics loaded her onto a gurney.

"What happened?"

Luke turned to find Ace running toward him, followed by Ry, Rory, Woodrow and Whit. Ry broke away from the group and headed for the ambulance.

"I don't know," Luke said and gulped. "The cabin was filled with smoke, and Lauren was passed out on the floor of her bedroom. I broke the window and got her out." He gulped again, thinking how limp her body was, how lifeless, and turned his gaze to the ambulance. "I found a pulse. Weak, though. Gave her CPR. Then the paramedics came and took over."

Ace slung an arm around Luke's shoulders and watched with him as Lauren was loaded into the ambulance. "Ry's going with them," Ace said. "He'll see that she gets the care she needs."

Too choked by emotion to speak, Luke could only nod.

The ambulance sped off, lights flashing and siren wailing. It had no sooner disappeared from sight than a fire truck appeared.

Volunteer firefighters spilled from the truck on to the ground and began dragging out equipment. A ladder was placed against the side of the cabin, and one of the men climbed up. Luke stood with the Tanner brothers and watched as the man worked his way over to the chimney and peered down. He flipped up the helmet that protected his face and called something to one of the men on the ground, who then climbed the ladder to join him. Using the long tool the second man had brought with him, they fed its length down the chimney. After a few minutes of maneuvering, they began to pull the tool out. When it cleared the chimney's opening, Luke saw that a smoldering blanket dangled from its end.

Luke turned to Ace, his face taut with fury. "Somebody tried to kill her. Blocked the chimney so the cabin would fill up with smoke."

Ace nodded grimly. "Sure looks that way."

Luke spun for the woods. Ace caught his arm and hauled him back. "Where are you going?"

"To find the son of a bitch who did this."

When Luke would've jerked free, Ace tightened his grip. "Wait a minute. You can't go off half-cocked like this. You don't know what you're up against. The man could be armed."

"I've got my gun. Used its butt to break the window."

"We'll call the sheriff," Ace said. "Let the law handle this."

Luke jerked free. "To hell with the law! Whoever did this will be long gone before the sheriff could get here. I'm going to find who did this to Lauren and make him pay."

Woodrow moved to stand with him. "You won't go alone." He glanced over at his brothers. "We're going with you. This is our fight, too."

Luke inhaled a breath through his nose, fighting back the need to handle this himself. With the Tanners' help, his chances of tracking down the culprit were increased five-fold. "All right," he said, releasing the breath. "This is how we'll play it. I'll take the area directly behind the cabin. Woodrow, you take the woods to the left. Ace, you and Rory make a sweep from the right. We'll meet up at the barn when we're done. If anybody finds anything, squeeze off a shot, and the rest will come runnin'." He set his jaw. "And when we find the son of a bitch, he's mine. Understand?"

Whatever weariness Luke had felt prior to finding Lauren was gone. Every nerve in his body was fully alert and focused on tracking down the man who had hurt her. He worked his way through the woods, his ears cocked to hear the slightest sound, his eyes narrowed to detect the barest movement. Five hundred acres surrounded the cabin, and Luke was prepared to crawl over the entire area on his hands and knees, if need be, to find the person responsible for hurting Lauren.

Thankfully, he was familiar with the terrain. The land butted the Bar-T, and Luke had spent many a day searching for cattle that had strayed from Tanner land and onto that which surrounded the lodge. While he walked, his gun at the ready, he tried to think of all the places a person might hide. There were hundreds of gullies, natural washes that rain and time had carved into the land, where a man could hide. And there were literally thousands of trees with brush underneath tall enough to conceal a full-grown deer.

But knowing that searching for the man was like looking for a needle in a haystack didn't slow Luke or lessen his determination to find him. He'd find the man who hurt Lauren and make him pay.

A sound stopped him in his tracks, and he lifted his head, listening. He closed his eyes, silently identifying the usual sounds of the forest, until he heard the strange noise again. It was human, he was sure. The deranged cackle a crazy person would make.

Hunkering down low, he made his way through the thicket, using the barrel of his gun to push back the vines that blocked his path. Hearing the sound again, he sank to his heels and listened. Though faint, the sound wasn't a product of his imagination. Someone was definitely out there.

Frowning, he lifted his nose and sniffed the air. Smoke. A campfire? Setting his jaw, he heaved himself up and pushed on, following the scent of smoke. Before him lay a gully, he knew. Deeper than the others that traversed the land, it was fed by the overflow from the pond just on the other side of the woods. He'd roped many a steer and dragged it to safety after the animal had gotten too close to the gully's edge and fallen in. He wished he had his horse and a rope with him now. He'd like nothing better than to rope the son of a bitch hiding there and drag him out. Only, he wouldn't stop when the man cleared the side. He'd keep dragging, filling the man's hide with the needles of the cactus that peppered the land and busting his bones against the rocks that jutted from the escarpment.

Pleased by the thought of the man's suffering, Luke stretched out on his stomach and peered over the edge of the gully. He could see the faint glow of the campfire, make out the shape of a crude shelter, fashioned from tree limbs and long blades of grass, in the stingy light it offered. But he didn't see any signs of life. Confident that whoever had built the fire was in the shelter, he braced his hands against the ground and started to heave himself up.

A blow to the back of his head sent him sprawling on his stomach again. Blinded by pain, he rolled to his left and missed receiving a second blow by mere inches. Shaking his head to clear his vision, he saw a man bearing down on him, a length of firewood gripped between his hands. Luke leaped to his feet, holding his arms out, poised for battle. His shotgun lay on the ground to his left but was too far away for him to make a dive for it.

Knowing he had to rely on his strength and his wits, he began to circle the man, measuring his opponent. The guy had to be pushing sixty, but was nimble and strong.

"Who are you?" Luke growled. "What do you have against Lauren?"

The man cackled again, the sound that of a madman, and took a swing. Luke jumped back, sucking in his stomach, to dodge the blow.

"Name don't matter," the man said, circling right along with Luke. "The woman stole my place and I'm gettin' it back."

"The lodge isn't yours," Luke told him. "It was built by the Tanners, and it's Lauren's now."

The man curled his lip, then spat on the ground. "Randall's whelp. Buck warned me his brother might try to take it one day."

Hoping to keep the man talking long enough to work

his way around to his gun, Luke snorted. "A man can't take what he already owns. Buck's daddy willed the lodge to Randall."

"Shoulda never split up the land. It's Tanner land and shoulda gone to Buck, like the rest of it did."

"Buck got his share and then some," Luke reminded him. "Randall was entitled to a part of the Tanner estate."

The man shook his head, his eyes wild. "Buck was the firstborn. By law, it shoulda been his."

"And what law is that?" Luke taunted, and edged another step closer to his gun. "*Buck's* law?"

"God's law, dammit! Bible states clear as can be that the firstborn son inherits the land."

"Did Buck tell you that? Or did you read it yourself?"

"Don't matter. It's the law."

Out of his peripheral vision, Luke glimpsed his shotgun. Eight more steps, maybe ten, and it would be within his reach.

"Buck's dead," Luke reminded the man. "Even if you managed to get the land away from Lauren, it would pass to his sons, not you."

The man spit again. "Bunch of sissies," he growled. "Don't possess between 'em the gonads their daddy had. They'd roll over and beg, 'fore they'd stand and fight for what's theirs."

"I wouldn't be so sure of that."

The old man jumped, then whirled to find Ace standing behind him, a rifle aimed at his chest.

"Hello, Claude," Ace said, as if greeting an old friend. "Haven't seen you around since Buck's funeral. Me and my brothers thought, with Buck no longer around to bail you out of jail, you must've skipped the country."

The old man looked wildly around, then dove for Luke's shotgun. Luke dove at the same moment, but the old man was closer. Luke tried to scramble up, but the old man pushed the barrel against his chest and forced him back down.

His smile smug, the old man glanced over at Ace. "Wanna see who can squeeze off the first shot? I'm bettin', when the smoke clears, your friend here'll be dead, and I'll still be standin', 'cause you ain't got the guts to kill a man."

Woodrow stepped from the woods to stand beside Ace, the stock of his gun braced against his shoulder, the old man in its sights. "If he doesn't, I sure as hell do."

"So do I," Rory said, as he joined his brothers.

Luke watched the panic fill the man's eyes as Whit stepped from the woods. A split second later, the old man was swinging the shotgun around and pointing it at the Tanners.

Knowing that at least one of the brothers was bound to catch a bullet if he didn't do something, Luke heaved himself from the ground and bowed his head, driving it into the old man's stomach. The gun went off, echoing around them, as they hit the ground. Luke quickly sat up and clamped a hand around the man's throat, holding him down.

"Y'all all right?" he shouted over his shoulder.

"Fine," Ace reported, then blew out a shaky breath. "But I might need to change my shorts later."

Ten

Lauren blinked open her eyes, then let them drift closed again.

"Lauren?"

The voice seemed to come from a long way away and threatened the darkness that cocooned her.

"Lauren."

She squirmed, trying to escape the voice's insistence.

"Lauren. Wake up."

Finally the voice pierced the fog that clogged her mind. Recognizing it, she turned away and curled herself into a ball. "Go away, Ry," she moaned. "I don't want you here."

"Lauren, I need you to open your eyes."

"Can't," she mumbled, then wet her dry lips. "Too heavy."

"Are you thirsty?"

She nodded her head. "Mouth's dry." Wincing, she placed a hand at her throat. Her voice wasn't right. It sounded hoarse, and speaking made her throat hurt.

Something cold and wet bumped her lips, and she parted them to accept the piece of ice, sucked on it greedily.

"Do you know where you are?" Ry asked.

Frowning, she forced open one eye. Seeing nothing familiar, she closed it again. "No."

"You're in the hospital. In ICU."

She opened her eyes and stared, seeing the white wall, the equipment crowded against the bed she lay on. Fear tightened her chest. "What happened?"

"You don't remember?"

She shook her head, then rolled to her back and looked up at Ry, remembering. "Smoke. I woke up and my bedroom was filled with smoke."

He nodded soberly. "Yes, it was."

"Was there a fire?" She pressed a hand to her forehead and the ache there. "I thought it was a dream."

"There wasn't a fire," he assured her. "Just smoke. Someone stuffed a wet blanket down your chimney, blocking it so that it wouldn't draw. With nowhere else to go, the smoke filled the cabin."

She pressed her hand to her chest, remembering the sensation of smothering. "I couldn't breathe. I crawled to the bathroom to wet a towel to cover my face." She frowned again, trying to remember. "I was going to break the window." She looked up at Ry. "Did I? Is that how I got out?"

He shook his head. "No. Luke broke the window and carried you out."

She closed her eyes at the mention of Luke and gulped, then forced them open again. "Is he all right?"

Smiling, he laid his hand over hers. "He's fine. He caught the man responsible. I'm ashamed to say it was an old friend of Buck's. He's in jail now. He won't be bothering you again."

She tried to sit up. "The lodge," she croaked, panicking. "The hunters are coming."

He pressed her back down. "They're already here. And don't worry. They're being taken care of. My brothers and their wives are at the lodge now, helping." He chuckled softly. "And from what I've heard, Rhena is keeping them hopping."

She stared, shocked by the kindness. "I…I don't know what to say."

"You don't need to say anything. Family takes care of family."

She gulped, ashamed of her treatment of her cousins. "Luke," she said, realizing that she'd treated him just as badly.

"He's out in the waiting room. Been there hours waiting for you to wake up."

Tears filled her eyes and she tried to sit up again. "I need to see him. Talk to him."

Ry pressed a hand against her chest and gently forced her back down. "I'll get him for you, but you have to promise that you won't get excited or upset. You had a close brush with death, and you need to remain quiet and give your lungs a chance to heal."

She nodded. "I promise. I just need to see him. Touch him." Her lips trembling, she gripped Ry's arm. "Please. I just want to see him."

Luke sat in one of the chairs in the waiting room, his elbows braced on his knees and his face buried in his hands. He wasn't sure how much more of this uncertainty he could take before he started tearing the hospital apart with his bare hands. They wouldn't let him see her. Rules, they'd said. Only immediate family members were allowed to visit patients in the ICU.

He dropped his hands and shoved back in the chair, scowling. And he was sick to death of hearing the word *stable.* Every time he asked one of the nurses about Lauren's condition, they replied with, "Stable." What the hell kind of word was that? What did it *mean?* If they'd let him see her, he'd be able to judge her condition for himself.

"Rules," he muttered under his breath, then pushed to his feet and headed for the nurses' station. As far as he was concerned, they could take their damn rules and shove them where the sun didn't shine. He was going to see Lauren, and anybody who got in his way was gonna get mowed down.

Just as he reached the nurses' station, Ry stepped from the ICU. Paling, Luke rushed toward him. "Is she okay? Has something happened to her?"

Smiling, Ry slung an arm around his shoulders. "Why don't you see for yourself? She just woke up."

Luke glanced over his shoulder, expecting the sour-faced nurse at the desk to try to stop him.

Chuckling, Ry opened the door. "That's the good thing about having a doctor for a friend. Doctors can open doors lower mortals can't."

Shooting Ry a frown, Luke stepped through the door, then paused outside the cubicle that housed Lauren, afraid to take that first step inside. He could see her through the glass wall that separated them. She looked so small, lying there, her face nearly as white as the sheet that covered her. Her eyes were closed and an oxygen tube was inserted into her nostrils. Another tube trailed from the IV bottle hanging from a pole beside her to a needle inserted in the back of her left hand.

Hearing the rhythmic beat of the heart monitor and the gentle shush of the oxygen tank as it forced air into her lungs thrust him back to the months he'd spent in a cubicle like this and all the pain he'd endured. Tears filled his eyes. Even knowing that, he'd trade places with her in a heartbeat and suffer it all again, if it would spare her any pain.

Aware that his time with her was limited, he dragged a sleeve across his eyes, then eased open the door and stepped inside. Not wanting to wake her, he tiptoed to the side of the bed, satisfied to simply look at her. Tears welled in his eyes again and he stubbornly fought them back. He wouldn't cry over losing her. Crying wouldn't do either of them any good. But, God, he needed to touch her, hold her. Convince himself that she was all right.

Cautiously he lifted a hand and brushed his knuckles across her cheek. Her eyes fluttered open and she met his gaze.

"Luke."

He gulped, swallowed, then drew his hand back, unsure how she felt about him being there. "You okay?"

She nodded and smiled softly. "Thanks to you."

He ducked his head, afraid she'd see the emotion in his eyes. "I'm just thankful I got to you in time."

He felt the brush of her fingers on his hand and looked up to see her smiling at him. Unable to help himself, he laced his fingers with hers and clung.

"I was dreaming about you," she said, and the hoarseness of her voice nearly brought him to his knees.

"The barn was burning and you ran out of it, your clothes on fire. I ran to help you. But no matter how hard I ran, I couldn't reach you."

"Don't talk," he urged. "You're gonna make your throat hurt worse."

She shook her head. "I have to tell you about it. It was the dream that woke me. At first, when I saw the smoke that filled my room, I thought I was still dreaming."

He squeezed her hand, not wanting to think how close she'd come to death. "Lauren. Don't. Please."

"But I wasn't dreaming." She paused to wet her lips, then continued. "I know what it must have been like for you inside that barn. The smoke. How it burns your throat and lungs. The sense of being smothered and the helplessness you must have experienced, knowing there was nothing you could do to give yourself air."

"Lauren, please," he begged.

"But I don't know what it feels like to have my skin burn," she said, ignoring him. "Or what it's like to go through the awful treatments you went through to have the charred flesh scraped away."

He dipped his chin and sent up a thankful prayer that she wouldn't have to go through that kind of pain or suffer the kind of scarring the fire had left him with.

"Luke?"

He lifted his head to meet her gaze and felt a moment's panic when he saw the tears in her eyes. "Are you in pain? Do I need to call the nurse?"

She shook her head and drew their joined hands to hold against her cheek. "I'm so sorry, Luke," she said tearfully. "For all the things I said to you."

He released a long breath. "No. You were right to say those things. I deceived you."

"But it wasn't to harm me," she told him. "You were only doing as you were asked. You were looking out for me."

"That doesn't make what I did right. It was wrong and I knew it."

She searched his face, then asked hesitantly, "Was loving me part of the deception?"

Desperate to convince her that it wasn't, he dropped to a knee, putting himself at eye level with her. "No. Never. I swear. What happened between us—" He dropped his gaze, trying to think of the words he needed to express his feelings. When he lifted his gaze to look at her again, tears blurred her image. "I've never been any good at stringing together words, but making love with you was beautiful. Sacred even. It was my way of showing you how much I cared for you. How much I loved you. I couldn't fake that kind of emotion. I wouldn't even know how."

"Oh, Luke," she said tearfully. "I was so afraid I'd destroyed whatever feelings you might've had for me, with all the ugly things I said." She reached to touch him, but the IV tube stopped her short. She gave it a frustrated tug, trying to get more length.

He sprang to his feet and caught her hand, forcing it back to her side. "Don't. You're going to hurt yourself."

She scooted over, making room for him on the bed beside her. "Climb up here with me."

He glanced at the door, sure that the nurse would come barreling in and throw him out on his ear, if she were to catch him on the bed. "I shouldn't," he said hesitantly. "It's probably against hospital rules."

"Screw the rules," she said impatiently. "I want to hold you."

Wanting the same damn thing, Luke toed off his boots and climbed onto the bed beside her. After carefully arranging the tubes and wires attached to her, he slipped an arm beneath her shoulders and drew her to his side.

She settled with a sigh, her head resting on his shoulder. Luke was certain he'd never known such contentment, as he felt with her in his arms.

"I love you, Luke," she whispered.

He pressed a kiss to the top of her head. "No more than I love you."

Growing pensive, she trailed a finger over his chest. "Luke?"

"Hmm?"

"I know that this isn't usually the way things are done, but—"

Frowning, he placed a finger beneath her chin and forced her gaze to his. "But what?"

"Would you marry me?"

His eyes bugged. "Marry you?"

She sat up. "Yes, marry me. I know that you're sort of old-fashioned and would probably rather do the asking yourself, but, well, if I wait for you to propose, there's no telling how long it would take you to work up the nerve, and I don't want to take a chance on you changing your mind about the way you feel about me."

Biting back a smile, he heaved himself up to sit beside her. "I'm not going to change my mind, Lauren. I've waited this many years to fall in love with a woman, I doubt I'll fall out of love anytime soon."

Her look of confusion was so comical, it was all he could do not to laugh. "What?" he asked.

"I'm trying to figure out if that was a yes or a no."

Chuckling, he wrapped his arms around her and gathered her close. "No, I'm not going to change my mind, and, yes, I'll marry you."

She went limp in his arms. "Thank God," she said weakly. "I don't know what I would've done if your yes and no had been reversed."

Laughing, he hugged her against his chest. "Maybe we should consider hiring an interpreter."

She pressed a finger to his lips. "I hate to tell you this, but I'm not one of the rich Tanners. We can't afford to hire an interpreter. Rhena will just have to do. She seems to understand you better than I do, anyway."

He sank back against the pillows, holding Lauren to his chest, and searched her face, trying to figure out what a beautiful woman like her would see in an old, scar-faced cowboy like him. Finding nothing but love in her eyes, he heaved a contented sigh. "I am one lucky man."

Smiling, she snuggled close. "We're both lucky. We found each other, didn't we?"

"The Tanner ties," he said thoughtfully, realizing how much more he was indebted to the Tanner family now. If not for the lodge and the Tanner brothers' relation to Lauren, he never would've met the love of his life.

"Who'd have ever thought…" Lauren said with a sigh.

* * * * *

*Look for an exciting new miniseries
from Peggy Moreland
coming summer 2006!*

If you enjoyed what you just read,
then we've got an offer you can't resist!

Take 2 bestselling love stories FREE!

Plus get a FREE surprise gift!

Clip this page and mail it to Silhouette Reader Service™

IN U.S.A.	IN CANADA
3010 Walden Ave.	P.O. Box 609
P.O. Box 1867	Fort Erie, Ontario
Buffalo, N.Y. 14240-1867	L2A 5X3

YES! Please send me 2 free Silhouette Desire® novels and my free surprise gift. After receiving them, if I don't wish to receive anymore, I can return the shipping statement marked cancel. If I don't cancel, I will receive 6 brand-new novels every month, before they're available in stores! In the U.S.A., bill me at the bargain price of $3.80 plus 25¢ shipping and handling per book and applicable sales tax, if any*. In Canada, bill me at the bargain price of $4.47 plus 25¢ shipping and handling per book and applicable taxes**. That's the complete price and a savings of at least 10% off the cover prices—what a great deal! I understand that accepting the 2 free books and gift places me under no obligation ever to buy any books. I can always return a shipment and cancel at any time. Even if I never buy another book from Silhouette, the 2 free books and gift are mine to keep forever.

225 SDN DZ9F
326 SDN DZ9G

Name	(PLEASE PRINT)	
Address	Apt.#	
City	State/Prov.	Zip/Postal Code

Not valid to current Silhouette Desire® subscribers.

**Want to try two free books from another series?
Call 1-800-873-8635 or visit www.morefreebooks.com.**

* Terms and prices subject to change without notice. Sales tax applicable in N.Y.
** Canadian residents will be charged applicable provincial taxes and GST.
All orders subject to approval. Offer limited to one per household.
® are registered trademarks owned and used by the trademark owner and or its licensee.

DES04R   ©2004 Harlequin Enterprises Limited

Don't miss the newest installment of
DYNASTIES : THE ASHTONS

A family built on lies...brought together
by dark, passionate secrets.

THE HIGHEST BIDDER
by Roxanne St. Claire

Paige Ashton never expected to be thrust into the
spotlight as a "bachelorette" during the fund-raising
auction she's coordinating. She certainly didn't
expect bachelor Matt Camberlane to bid on her...or
the startling passion that erupted between them.

Available October 2005 from Silhouette Desire.

COMING NEXT MONTH

#1681 THE HIGHEST BIDDER—Roxanne St. Claire
Dynasties: The Ashtons
A sexy millionaire bids on a most unlikely bachelorette and gets the surprise of his life.

#1682 DANGER BECOMES YOU—Annette Broadrick
The Crenshaws of Texas
Two strangers find themselves snowbound and looking for ways to stay warm, while staying out of danger.

#1683 ROUND-THE-CLOCK TEMPTATION—
Michele Celmer
Texas Cattleman's Club: The Secret Diary
This tough Texan bodyguard is offering his protection…day and night!

#1684 A SCANDALOUS MELODY—Linda Conrad
The Gypsy Inheritance
She'll do anything to keep her family's business…even become her enemy's mistress.

#1685 SECRET NIGHTS AT NINE OAKS—Amy J. Fetzer
When a wealthy recluse hides from the world, only one woman can save him from his self-imposed exile.

#1686 WHEN THE LIGHTS GO DOWN—Heidi Betts
Plain Jane gets a makeover and a lover who wants to turn their temporary tryst into a permanent arrangement.

SDCNM0905